The Beach

ALEX GARLAND

Level 6

Retold by Joanna Strange
Series Editors: Andy Hopkins and Jocelyn Potter

Pearson Education Limited
Edinburgh Gate, Harlow,
Essex CM20 2JE, England
and Associated Companies throughout the world.

ISBN 0 582 43567 6

First published by Viking 1996
This edition first published 2001

3 5 7 9 10 8 6 4 2

Original copyright © Alex Garland 1996
Text copyright © Penguin Books 2001

Typeset by Ferdinand Pageworks, London
Set in 11/14pt Bembo
Printed in Spain by Mateu Cromo, S. A. Pinto (Madrid)

Published by Pearson Education Limited in association with
Penguin Books Ltd, both companies being subsidiaries of Pearson Plc

For a complete list of the titles available in the Penguin Readers series please write to your local
Pearson Education office or to: Marketing Department, Penguin Longman Publishing,
80 Strand, London, WC2R 0RL

Contents

Introduction

'Close your eyes and think about a lagoon hidden from the sea and passing boats by a high, curving wall of rock. Then imagine idyllic white sands and coral gardens ... On the white sands, fishing in the coral gardens, is a select group of travellers ...'

Richard, a young backpacker from England, arrives in Thailand looking for adventure. He isn't an ordinary tourist – tourists just go on holiday. Richard is a traveller, and travellers are always searching for new experiences in unknown places.

At a cheap guest-house in Bangkok, Richard hears about 'the Beach', on a secret island somewhere in the Gulf of Thailand. It sounds like paradise on earth. He sets off on a journey with a French couple, Étienne and Françoise, to find the Beach and the small community of travellers who live on it.

But this heaven on earth is not what it seems. A series of tragic events soon turns paradise into hell ...

The Beach is author Alex Garland's first novel. Garland was born in London in 1970 and began his career as an artist before writing *The Beach* in 1996. The novel won a prize in 1997, and has sold over five million copies worldwide. Garland's second novel, *The Tesseract*, was published in 1999.

The film of *The Beach* stars the famous American actor Leonardo DiCaprio as Richard, and the French actress Virginie Ledoyen as Françoise. It is directed by Danny Boyle. The film was made in Thailand, famous for its unspoilt islands and idyllic beaches.

Chapter 1   Bangkok

The first time I heard of the beach was in Bangkok, on the Khao San Road. Khao San Road was backpacker land. Almost all the buildings were guest-houses for travellers on their way into or out of Thailand; it was a place between East and West.

I'd landed in Bangkok from England in the late afternoon. As soon as the taxi dropped me on the Khao San Road, I caught the smell of dope. Half the travellers wandering past me were stoned.

I found a cheap guest-house easily, and a quarter of an hour later I was settling into a room that was only slightly larger than a double bed. The walls were dirty and bare and stopped before they reached the ceiling, so I could hear everything in the rooms on each side of me. On the ceiling was a fan, and for a while I just lay on the bed and looked up at it. It was calming, and the mixture of the heat and the gentle noise of the fan soon sent me to sleep.

I slept deeply until I heard the man's footsteps in the corridor. They were different, too weird to sleep through. They dragged on the floor, and a stream of British swear-words floated into my room as the man tried to unlock his door. Then his light came on and, frowning, I looked at my watch. It was two in the morning – early evening in England – and I wondered if I would ever manage to get back to sleep.

The man coughed, then I heard him rolling a joint. Soon there was blue smoke caught in the light above the dividing wall.

'Bitch,' said a voice suddenly. 'I could be dead.'

The voice paused while the man coughed. I was wide awake now.

'Cancer in the coral, blue water, my bitch. Nearly killed me,' the man continued.

1

He had an accent, but at first I couldn't think where he came from.

'*Bitch*,' he said again, spitting out the word.

A Scottish accent. Beach.

Then suddenly the man's head appeared in the gap between my wall and the ceiling.

'Hey,' he said.

I didn't move. I was sure he couldn't see me.

'Hey. I know you're listening in there. I know you're awake. Here.'

Something sailed through the darkness and landed on my bed. The joint he'd been smoking. I grabbed it to stop it burning the sheets.

Holding up the joint I asked, 'Do you want this back?'

'You *were* listening,' he replied, ignoring me. 'You heard me talking about the beach. Tell me what you heard.'

'I didn't hear anything.'

'You're lying. You were listening,' he shouted.

I thought he was going to shout at me all night, but he suddenly seemed to change his mind and his head disappeared. I heard him light another joint and then he switched off his light.

I hardly slept for the rest of the night, and went downstairs to the eating area early to get some breakfast. When I got back to my room, I found an envelope pinned to my door. On it was written: *Here is the map*.

A couple of minutes later, I was sitting on my bed with the ceiling fan cooling the back of my neck and the map in my hands. It was carefully drawn and beautifully coloured in. At the top of the map were the words *Gulf of Thailand* in thick red ink. Below them were several small islands. On one of them I noticed a black mark. An X. I looked closer. Written underneath, in tiny letters, was the word *Beach*.

The man in the next room! He must have pinned the map on

my door. I wasn't sure exactly what I was going to say to him. I was curious, that's all. I just wanted to know what was so special about this beach. His door was unlocked. I listened outside for a minute before knocking, and when I did the door swung open.

It was dark in the room, but there was just enough light for me to see. The man was lying on the bed, looking up at the ceiling. I think he'd cut his wrists. Or it could have been his neck. In the dark, with so much blood splashed about, it was hard to tell what he'd cut. But I knew he'd done the cutting: there was a knife in his hand.

I stood still, staring at the body for a couple of minutes. Then I went to get help.

◆

The policeman was sweating, but not with the heat. It was the effort of speaking English. When he came to a difficult word or a complicated sentence he would stop and wipe the sweat from his forehead.

'Mr Duck your friend, yes?' he asked.

I shook my head. 'I'd never met him before last night. And listen; Daffy Duck can't be his real name. It's a joke name.'

'Joke name?' said the policeman.

'Not a true name,' I explained. 'Daffy Duck is a character in a children's film. Like Bugs Bunny or Mickey Mouse.'

'Ah, so dead man gives false name to guest-house,' said the policeman, when he finally understood what I was saying. 'OK. Last night. In hotel. Tell me again.'

I didn't tell the policeman about the map. I didn't want to get involved in a police investigation and spoil my holiday. I don't think the policeman cared about the dead man much anyway, because after about thirty minutes he let me go.

As I left the police station, I saw a French boy who I'd met in the guest-house at breakfast. He and his girlfriend, Françoise, had a room on the other side of the dead man's and they'd been brought to the police station for questioning too. I sat down next to Étienne in the sun on the steps of the police station. The death was an unusual start to the day and I needed to talk to someone about it.

'Hi,' I said. 'Do you speak English?'

'Hi. Yeah, sure, I speak English. You're the one who found the dead guy, aren't you?'

'Yes, I found him this morning,' I said, pulling my cigarettes out of my pocket. 'Do you smoke?'

'No thanks. My name's Étienne, by the way.'

'I'm Richard,' I said, and we shook hands. 'This is so weird. I only arrived in Thailand last night. I wanted to relax in Bangkok, if that's possible, and instead I found a dead man!'

'Well, we've been here for four weeks but it's weird for us too.'

'So where have you been for the last month? Not only in Bangkok, surely?'

'Oh no. We've been in the north. Chiang Mai. Walking in the hills and rafting on a river. Very boring, no?'

'Boring?' I asked, surprised.

'Yeah. I wanted to do something different. All travellers want to do something different but in the end we all do the same thing. There's no ... ah ...'

'Adventure.'

'Yes. We come to Thailand for an adventure but all we find is this,' he said, pointing down the Khao San Road.

'This dead man,' he continued after a few seconds. 'He was very strange. He used to talk about a beach every night.'

'I know where the beach is,' I said. Étienne looked interested. 'I've got a map. He drew it for me. I found it pinned to my door this morning. It shows where the beach is and how to get there. I've got it in my room.'

'Did you tell the police?' Étienne asked.

'No, I didn't want to get involved. Maybe they'd think I knew him or something but I didn't. I'd never met him before last night.'

'A map,' said Étienne quietly. 'Cool. Can I see it?'

'Yeah, sure. But what about your girlfriend? She's still with the police, isn't she?'

'Françoise? Oh, she'll be all right. She knows the way back to the guest-house.'

'OK then,' I said. 'Let's go.'

When we got back to my room, Étienne stared at the map for five minutes without speaking. Then he said, 'Wait,' and ran out of the room. He came back holding a guidebook. 'There,' he said, pointing to an open page. 'These are the islands on the map. They're in a national marine park west of Ko Samui and Ko Pha-Ngan. All the islands are protected. Tourists aren't allowed to visit them. They can go to one, Ko Phelong, on a special guided tour from Ko Samui but they can only stay one night. And they can't leave the island.'

'So Mr Duck's beach is in a national park. How do people get there?' I asked.

'They can't get there. That's the point.'

I leant back on my bed and lit a cigarette. 'Well, Mr Duck's map is rubbish then.'

Étienne shook his head. 'No. Not rubbish. Why do you think the man drew it so carefully and gave it to you?'

'He was crazy. He called himself Daffy Duck,' I laughed.

'I don't think he was mad. Maybe travellers try to get to new islands in the national park because islands like Ko Samui and Ko Pha-Ngan are spoilt. Too many tourists.'

'But they aren't allowed in the national park,' I said.

Étienne raised his eyes to the ceiling. 'Exactly! That's why they go there. You know, Richard, I'd like to find this beach.'

I smiled.

'Really,' said Étienne. 'Believe me.'

I did believe him. He had a look in his eyes that I recognized. He wanted an adventure. I could tell that he was already listening to the sound of the waves on this idyllic beach, or hiding from the marine-park guides as he made his way to the island.

At that moment Françoise arrived. She was one of the most attractive girls I'd ever seen. I didn't want to seem impressed by her looks, so when she put her head round the door I just looked up, said 'Hi', then went back to studying the map.

Étienne spoke to her quickly in French. I couldn't follow the conversation but I recognized a few words, including my own name once or twice. I think she was annoyed that he'd left the police station without her. After some minutes their voices relaxed. Then Françoise said, 'May I have a cigarette, Richard?'

'Sure.' I gave her one and held out a light.

'So, what's this map then?' she asked.

'I found it on my door . . .' I started to explain.

'Yes, Étienne's already told me. Can I see it?'

I passed the map to her and Étienne pointed out the beach.

'Just a short boat ride from Ko Phelong,' he said.

'How do we know what we'll find there?' Françoise asked.

'We don't,' I replied.

'And if there's nothing there, how do we get back to Ko Samui?'

'We get back to Ko Phelong,' said Étienne. 'Then we wait for a tourist boat. We say we were lost. It'll be fine.'

'I see . . . OK . . . When are we leaving then?'

I looked at Étienne and he looked back at me.

'I'm tired of Bangkok,' Françoise continued. 'Let's get the night train south tonight.'

'Yeah, but . . .' I said slowly, surprised by the speed at which events were developing.

'We're going,' said Françoise, and put out her cigarette on the floor as if that was the end of the discussion. And it was.

♦

We took the night train south from Bangkok, first class. I didn't feel able to relax until I was in bed on the train, away from Étienne and Françoise. Things had been awkward since leaving the guest-house. I had no objection to their company, but I was beginning to think about the reality of our plans. Also, I realised that we were complete strangers – something I'd forgotten in the excitement of our quick decision to find the beach together. I'm sure they were feeling the same, which was why they were as quiet as I was.

At Surat Thani we got off the train and took a bus to Don Sak. From there we caught the Songserm ferry, straight to Na Thon. That was how we got to the tourist island of Ko Samui.

Chapter 2   Ko Samui

A bus from the Ko Samui port took us to the Chaweng beach resort. On the left the sea lay blue between rows of coconut trees, and on the right a jungle-covered slope rose steeply. The bus left us outside a decent-looking bunch of beach huts. Private showers, a bedside fan, and a restaurant that looked on to the sea. Our huts faced each other over a path lined with tropical flowers.

First, I went for a swim – that way I could get clean and get a suntan. I ran down to the sea, partly because the sand was so hot and partly because I always run into the sea. I'd been splashing around in the water for about fifteen minutes when Étienne and Françoise came down to join me. Françoise looked lovely in a white swimsuit. I wondered if Étienne noticed her beauty, or whether he'd got used to it.

'Will you come for a swim?' she asked.

'I am swimming, aren't I?'

'No,' said Étienne, pointing to the open sea. 'She means a real swim. Out there.'

We played a game as we swam out. Every ten metres we would each dive to the bottom of the sea and return with a handful of sand. I found the game strangely unpleasant. A metre underwater the warmth of the tropical sea would stop and it would suddenly turn cold. The further we swam, the blacker and finer the sand became. Soon the water at the bottom became too dark for me to see anything, and I could only kick out blindly with my legs until my hands sank into the sand.

'How far out shall we go?' I asked, when the sunbathers on the beach behind us looked like insects.

Étienne smiled. 'You would like to go back now?'

'You are tired, Richard?' Françoise asked, eyebrows raised. 'We can go back.'

'I'm fine,' I replied. 'Let's swim further.'

At five that afternoon the temperature cooled, the sky turned black and it rained heavily. I sat outside my hut, under the roof, watching the storm.

After some time two guys came racing up the beach, laughing and shouting. They ran up to the hut next to mine.

'Man!' one of them shouted. 'What a storm! Whoop!'

'Americans,' I thought.

They tried to get into their hut but the door was locked.

'Lost our key!' the guy with white-blond hair shouted at me. 'Can't get in!'

I nodded. 'Bad luck. Where did you lose it?'

'Down the beach, man! A long way from here! Hey, can we come and sit with you? You want to smoke a joint?'

'Sure,' I said.

'Excellent!'

The two of them ran over to my hut and introduced themselves.

'I'm Sammy,' said the one with white-blond hair. 'And this is Zeph. Cool name, huh?'

'Definitely,' I answered, as we shook hands.

Sammy started rolling a joint. We smoked and chatted and watched the lightning out at sea. They made me laugh with their funny jokes and stories. After a while we were too stoned to do anything except sit in silence and listen to the thunder.

An hour or two after dark, a tiny Thai woman came over from the restaurant and gave Zeph a spare key to their hut.

As I stood up to say goodnight Sammy said, 'Hey, nice meeting you! See you tomorrow, man.'

'Sure,' I said, and shut my door behind me.

◆

The next morning the sky was still cloudy. Rubbing the sleep from my eyes, I walked over the cool sand to the restaurant and found Étienne and Françoise eating breakfast. I ordered a fruit salad and sat down with them.

'Who did you meet last night?' asked Étienne, as I pulled up a chair. 'We saw you talking outside your hut.'

I pulled out a cigarette to kill time before breakfast arrived. 'A couple of Americans. Zeph and Sammy.'

Françoise nodded. 'Did you tell them about our beach?'

'No.' I lit my cigarette. 'I didn't.'

'You shouldn't tell people about our beach.'

'I didn't tell them.'

'It should be a secret.'

'That's why I didn't tell them, Françoise,' I answered.

Étienne interrupted, smiling nervously. 'She was worried you might have . . .'

'I didn't even think of it,' I replied, annoyed, and put out my cigarette hard.

When breakfast came, I made an effort to relax and told them some of the Americans' jokes. Françoise thought they were extremely funny. Her laughter improved the atmosphere, and we began making plans for the day ahead.

We decided that we had to hire a boat. We couldn't hire one from the normal travel agencies because tourists weren't allowed to go to the islands in the marine park. Instead we would need to find a fisherman who was unaware or unconcerned about the marine park rules.

After breakfast, we set off up the beach. It didn't take us long to find a fisherman who agreed to take us to the marine park.

'That can be arranged,' he said, smiling at us. 'Of course, yes. Not difficult for me to do that.'

He looked at the map in Étienne's guidebook.

'Actually, my friend, your book is not correct. You can stay Ko

10

Phelong one night, two nights – is OK. But this island you can only stay one night.' He took Étienne's book and pointed to an island close to Ko Phelong.

Étienne looked at me and smiled. From my memory of Mr Duck's map, the island that the fisherman was pointing at was next to our beach island.

'OK,' said Étienne. 'But we want to stay more than one night. That is possible?'

The fisherman looked over his shoulder. 'Yes,' he whispered. 'But is more money, you understand?'

Étienne and the fisherman eventually agreed a price for the boat ride, and we arranged to meet him at six the next morning in the restaurant. He would take us to the island next to our beach island and, three nights later, he would collect us and bring us back to Ko Samui.

That left us with a couple of problems. How were we going to get to our beach island? And if we did manage to get there, we would be missing when the fisherman came to collect us.

Étienne and Françoise seemed much less concerned about these problems than I was. They had a simple solution to the first problem – we would swim. By examining Mr Duck's map and the map in their guidebook, they'd decided that the islands were about a kilometre apart. According to them, we could swim that distance. I wasn't so confident, remembering the diving game from the day before. The tide had pulled us a long way down Chaweng beach as we swam. If the same thing happened between the islands, the length of the swim could double.

Sunset was marvellous that evening. Étienne, Françoise and I were lying on the beach, watching the red sky gently fading to deep blue, when Zeph and Sammy came over to join us. We all got stoned together and went on watching the changing colours in the sky as if we were watching television.

11

'Hey,' Zeph said, waking us from our dreams. 'Have you heard the story about the beach?'

I shook my head.

'An amazing beach hidden somewhere but no one knows where it is.'

'No,' I said, 'we haven't. Tell us.'

'OK,' said Zeph and lay back on the sand. 'Close your eyes and think about a lagoon hidden from the sea and passing boats by a high, curving wall of rock. Then imagine idyllic white sands and coral gardens. Waterfalls surrounded by thick jungle. Plants untouched for a thousand years, strangely coloured birds and monkeys in the trees. On the white sands, fishing in the coral gardens, is a select group of travellers. They leave if they want to, they return, the beach never changes.'

'Select?' I asked quietly, as if talking through a dream. Zeph's vision was magical.

'Special,' he replied. 'Only a few lucky travellers know where this beach is.'

'It's paradise,' Sammy whispered.

'Paradise,' Zeph agreed, 'is what it sounds like.'

Françoise suddenly stood up. She was very worried that Zeph and Sammy knew about the beach.

'Now,' she said, dusting sand off her legs, 'we leave early tomorrow morning, for, ah, for Ko Pha-Ngan. So I think we shall eat and go to bed now. Étienne? Richard? Come.'

'Huh?' I said. 'Françoise, it's only seven-thirty in the evening.'

'We leave early in the morning,' she repeated. 'Good night, Sammy and Zeph. It was very nice meeting you. And really, your beach, what a silly story!' She laughed loudly.

We said goodbye to Sammy and Zeph and all shook hands awkwardly. Then Étienne and I followed Françoise.

The atmosphere at dinner was very tense, but Françoise knew she'd behaved foolishly. When we said goodnight, she apologized.

'I don't know why but I was suddenly frightened they would want to come with us,' she explained. 'I only want it to be us . . . Do you think they have realized we know about the beach?'

'Hard to say,' I answered. 'Everyone was stoned.'

Étienne nodded. 'Yes,' he said, and put his arm around Françoise's shoulder. 'Everyone was stoned. We should not worry.'

It took me a long time to get to sleep that night. It wasn't just because I was anxious about what might happen tomorrow. I was also troubled by the hurried way I'd said goodbye to Zeph and Sammy. I'd enjoyed their company and our parting had been too quick and awkward, too confused by dope and secrets. I felt there was something I'd left unsaid.

◆

In the cool early morning I got up and quickly drew Zeph and Sammy a map. There wasn't time to draw it as carefully as Mr Duck had. The islands were rough circles and there were only three labels – Ko Samui, Ko Phelong and Paradise. At the bottom of the page I wrote: *Wait on Chaweng for three days. If we haven't come back by then, it means we made it to the beach. See you there? Richard.*

I crept outside and slipped the map under Zeph and Sammy's door. Then I got my backpack, locked my hut and went to the restaurant to wait for Étienne and Françoise.

Chapter 3   Journey to Paradise

The morning sun played tricks in the sea. Gold shapes like fish spun beneath the surface. Sitting in the fisherman's yellow and white motor boat on our way to the island, I reached down and put my hand in the water. The fish swam in and out of my fingers.

I looked back at Ko Samui. Strangely it seemed far behind us, but the island we were going to still appeared as distant as it had an hour ago. I didn't move again until the water turned blue and I saw a coral bed beneath the boat. The fisherman turned off the engine.

'Now you pay,' he said, as we slid towards the shore of the island.

A few minutes later, I sat on the beach and watched the fisherman's boat slowly disappear into the distance, on its way back to Ko Samui. A few metres away, Étienne was studying the map. He was trying to work out which of the several islands near us was our beach island, the one we had to swim to. He didn't need my help, so I called to him that I was going to take a walk. I'd never been on a real desert island before – a deserted desert island – and I felt I ought to explore.

'Don't be long,' Étienne said. 'We should leave after lunch. We should not spend the night here.'

I started walking along the coast, looking for a place to turn inland. I eventually found some shady trees on the edge of a forest and sat down to smoke a cigarette.

Thinking about Thailand often makes me angry, and until I started writing this book I tried not to do it. I preferred it to stay hidden in the back of my mind. But I did think about Thailand sometimes, usually late at night. At those times I made an effort to remember sitting under those trees, smoking my cigarette. I chose this moment because it was the last time I could remember being me. Normal. Nothing much going through my head apart from how pretty the island was, and how quiet. It's hard to explain. I've been relying on an idea that these things would become clear to me as I wrote them down. It doesn't seem to be happening.

When I got back to the beach, I found Étienne making lunch.

I looked around. 'Where's Françoise?' I asked.

'She went to see how far it is to our island.'

When she came back, Françoise said our island was a kilometre away. To me, it just looked like a long swim.

'Are you sure we can do this?' I said, more to myself than anyone else.

'We can,' said Françoise.

'We can try,' Étienne corrected her.

We each took a few essential things from our backpacks and put them in strong plastic bags. The idea was that the bags would float on the water as we swam. They were strong enough to lean on, so we only had to swim with our legs. Then we hid our backpacks under some bushes.

At a quarter to four we were ready to leave. As we started to swim I heard Françoise say behind me, 'Maybe more than one kilometre.' Étienne said something in reply, but it was lost as a wave broke.

◆

The swim passed in stages. The first was full of confidence, chatting and making jokes about sharks. Then, as our legs began to ache, we stopped talking. The jokes about sharks became fears, and I started to doubt that I had the strength to finish the swim. We were about halfway between the two islands. Not being able to finish the swim would mean dying. And then, strangely, things

15

became easier. My legs seemed to kick automatically, allowing my mind to move beyond the pain. I was just thinking that I should try to pass my driving test if I got back to England, when I saw some wood on the beach ahead and realized we were nearly there.

When we reached the beach, we all fell exhausted on to the wet sand.

'We've done enough,' I said. 'We're staying here tonight.'

'But our special beach may be close, no?' said Étienne.

'Shh.'

♦

We set off immediately after breakfast. According to Mr Duck's map, the beach we were looking for was on the other side of the island. At first we walked along the coast, but the sand soon turned to sharp rocks. We realized we would have to go inland and find our way through the jungle.

The first two or three hundred metres from the shore were the hardest. The spaces between the trees were covered with strange bushes with small leaves that sliced our legs like razors. But as we got further inland and the ground began to rise, there were fewer plants on the forest floor and we found animal tracks that we could follow.

After two hours of walking, we found ourselves at the bottom of a particularly steep slope. Étienne was the first to reach the top.

'Hurry up!' he called enthusiastically. 'It is amazing.'

I climbed to the top next, leaving Françoise far behind. The slope led up to a shelf the size of a football pitch on the mountainside, so flat and neat that it seemed unnatural compared to the surrounding jungle. Étienne was ahead of me, standing in some bushy plants that looked familiar.

'Cool!' I said. 'Dope!'

Étienne grinned. 'Have you ever seen so much?'

16

'Never . . .' I pulled a few leaves from the nearest bush.

'We should pick some, Richard. We can dry it in the sun and . . .' Then he stopped. 'Wait a moment, there is something funny here.'

'What?'

'Well, it is just so . . . These plants . . .' His face turned white. 'This is a field.'

I froze. 'But it can't be a field. I mean, these islands are . . .'

'The plants are in rows.' We stared at each other. 'We are in deep trouble.'

Just then Françoise appeared, calling out to us.

'Hey! I have seen some people further up the mountain. They are coming this way. Maybe they are from our beach, no?'

I ran towards her. 'Shut up!' I said, putting my hand over her mouth. 'This is a dope field. Do you understand?'

Lying flat on the earth, looking through the leaves, we listened to the Thai voices getting closer and waited for people to appear. A man stepped into the field. He was young, maybe twenty. His chest was bare and we could see his strong muscles. He wore military trousers and held a gun in his hand. A second man appeared, also with a gun. They stopped and exchanged a few words. Then another man came out from the jungle and they set off again, down the slope we'd just climbed up.

Two or three minutes after their voices had faded away, Françoise suddenly burst into tears. Then Étienne started crying too. I watched the two of them blankly. The shock of discovering the fields and the tension while we'd been hiding had left me feeling empty.

Finally I managed to say, 'OK. We've got to leave. They might come back soon and find us.'

'Richard,' said Étienne. 'I do not want to die here. You must get us out.'

I must get them out? *Me*? I couldn't believe my ears! But just by looking at him, I could tell he wasn't going to take control of the situation. And neither was Françoise. She was staring at me with the same scared expression as Étienne.

So, having no choice, it was me who took the decision to go on.

I have almost no memory of the few hours after leaving the dope field. I think I was concentrating so hard on our immediate survival as we made our way down the other side of the mountain, that I can't remember anything until we reached the waterfall.

It was the height of a four-storey building – the kind of height I hate to stand upright near, so I crawled to the cliff edge on my stomach. On either side of the waterfall the cliff continued, eventually curving around into the sea, then, unbroken, rejoining the land on the far side. It was as if a huge circle had been cut out of the island to form a lagoon in a wall of rock – just as Zeph had described. From where we sat we could see that the cliffs were no more than thirty metres thick, but a passing boat could never guess what lay behind them. The water in the lagoon was presumably supplied by underwater caves and channels. The waterfall dropped into a pool from which a quick-flowing stream ran into the trees. Getting down into the pool was the problem.

'I think we've definitely found the right place,' I said to Étienne and Françoise, as I crawled back from the cliff edge. 'It's where Mr Duck's map says it is, and it fits Zeph's description perfectly.'

'Richard, there must be a way down, no?' said Françoise. 'If people go to the beach, there must be a way.'

'If people go to the beach,' I echoed. We hadn't seen any sign that people were down there. The beach looked beautiful but completely deserted.

'Maybe we can jump from the waterfall,' said Étienne.

I thought for a moment. 'Possibly,' I replied. I crawled back to the cliff edge and looked down at the pool. I stood up cautiously. 'OK,' I whispered to myself.

'Are you jumping?' called Étienne nervously.

'Just taking a better look,' I called back.

'So jump,' I heard my voice say. I paused, wondering if I'd heard myself correctly, and then I did. I jumped.

Everything happened as things are supposed to happen while one falls. I had time to think. Stupid things flashed through my head, like how my cat slipped off the kitchen table once and landed on its head. Then I hit the pool. It was so deep I never even touched the bottom.

'Ha!' I shouted, not caring who might hear. 'I'm alive!'

I looked up and saw Étienne and Françoise's heads looking over the cliff.

'You are OK?' called Étienne.

'I'm fine! I'm brilliant! Throw down the plastic bags!'

I sat on the grass and waited for Étienne and Françoise to jump. The man appeared just as I was lighting a cigarette. He walked out of the trees a few metres away from me. His skin was deeply sunburnt and he was wearing nothing except a pair of old blue shorts and a necklace made of sea shells. He had a full beard, which made it hard to tell his age, but I didn't think he was much older than me.

'Hey,' he said with his head on one side. 'You did the jump quickly for a newcomer.' His accent was English. 'It took me over an hour but I was alone so it was harder.'

Over the sound of the waterfall Étienne's voice called to me, saying he was going to jump. He wouldn't have been able to see the man. I didn't bother to answer him.

When Étienne and Françoise had both jumped, we followed the man through the trees. We didn't talk much as we walked. The only thing he would tell us was his name – Jed. He wouldn't answer the rest of our questions. 'Easier to talk at the camp,' he explained. 'We've got as many questions for you as you've got for us.'

At first glance, the camp was like I'd imagined it might be. There was a large, dusty clearing surrounded by trees, with some huts and a few tents. At the far end was a larger building, a longhouse, and beside it the stream from the waterfall reappeared.

I only noticed after looking at all this that there was something strange about the light. It was more like dusk than midday. I looked up, following the trunk of one of the huge trees. The lower branches had been cut away, but higher up the branches began to grow again, curving upwards over the clearing until they joined with the branches from the other side. They had formed a ceiling of wood and leaves over the clearing.

'We don't want to be seen from the air,' Jed explained. 'Planes sometimes fly over. Not often but sometimes.' He pointed upwards. 'Originally the branches were tied together with ropes but now they just grow that way. Clever, huh?'

'Amazing,' I agreed. I was so busy looking up that I didn't even notice that people had begun to come out of the longhouse and were walking across the clearing towards us. Three people to be exact. Two women and a man.

'Sal, Cassie and Bugs,' said one of the women in an American accent as they reached us. 'I'm Sal but don't try to remember our names.' She smiled warmly. 'You'll only get confused when you meet the others, and you'll learn them all eventually.'

I'm not likely to forget a name like Bugs, I thought to myself, managing not to laugh. I frowned and put a hand up to my forehead. Since jumping off the waterfall, my head had been feeling increasingly light. Now it had started to feel like it might float off my shoulders.

Françoise stepped up to the woman and said, 'Françoise, Étienne and Richard.'

'You're French! Lovely! We've only got one other French person here.'

'Richard is English,' Françoise said, pointing at me, and I tried to nod politely.

'Lovely!' said the woman again, watching me curiously out of the corner of her eye. 'Well, I know you're all hungry so let's get you some food.' She turned to the man. 'Bugs, can you make some soup? Then we can all have a long chat and get to know each other. Does that sound good?'

'It sounds great, Sal,' I said loudly. 'You know, you're quite right, I do feel hungry. We've only eaten . . .'

Jed ran to catch me as I fainted, but too late. As I fell backwards, the last thing I saw was a tiny bit of blue sky through the leafy ceiling. Then darkness rushed in.

◆

Late morning, I guessed. Only from the heat. In the darkness of the longhouse and the steady light of the candle, there was nothing else to reveal the time.

The woman called Sal sat at the foot of my bed. She was wearing a yellow T-shirt, and her long hair was tied back from her face. Around her neck was a necklace of sea shells.

'Finish it, Richard,' she said, looking at the bowl of fish soup that I held in my hands.

I lifted the bowl to my mouth then put it down again.

'I can't, Sal.'

'You must, Richard. You've had a bad fever.'

'I've finished most of it. Look.' I held up the bowl.

'OK,' she said, then folded her arms. 'Richard, we need to talk.'

We were alone in the longhouse. Occasionally I heard people enter and leave, but I couldn't see them. As I spoke Sal didn't interrupt me, frown, smile or nod. She just sat on the floor and listened. Soon I found myself talking to her as if she were a tape recorder or a priest. I told her everything that had happened since I arrived in Bangkok. When I told her about finding Mr

21

Duck's body, she looked sad. The only thing I didn't mention was that I'd given two other people directions to the island. I knew I should tell her about Zeph and Sammy, but I also thought she might be angry if she knew I'd spread the secret. Better to wait until I knew more about the camp and the other people who lived here.

At the end of my story she smiled. 'Well, Richard, it sounds like you had quite an adventure getting here.'

I waited for her to continue but she didn't.

'Uh, now can I ask you some questions, Sal?' I said quickly.

'I have some things to do, Richard,' she said, standing up.

'Just a few questions.'

She sat down again. 'OK. Five minutes.'

'Well . . . first I'd just like to know something about this place. I mean, what is it?'

'It's a beach resort. A place to come for vacations.'

I frowned. 'A beach resort?' I felt so disappointed. I was a traveller, not a tourist.

'What did you think this place was?' asked Sal.

'I don't know. I didn't think anything really. But I certainly didn't think it was just a beach resort.'

Sal waved a hand in the air. 'Well, OK, Richard. Of course this is more than a beach resort. We come here to relax by a beautiful beach but it isn't a beach resort because we're trying to get away from those sorts of places. Or we're trying to make a place that won't turn into one. See?'

'No.'

'You will see, Richard. It's not complicated.'

'How about the gunmen in the dope fields?' I asked. 'Are they anything to do with you?'

Sal shook her head. 'I have a feeling the fields are owned by ex-fishermen from Ko Samui but I could be wrong. They came to that half of the island a couple of years ago. We can't go there now.'

'But they know you're here.'

'Of course, but there isn't much they can do. They can't report us. If the marine park authorities came to look for us they'd find them too.'

'One more question,' I said, as she stood up to go. 'The man in Bangkok. Mr Duck. You knew him?'

'Yes,' she said quietly, then began walking away, 'he was a friend.'

'But . . . OK, just one more question. Where's the toilet?'

'Outside, second hut along by the edge of the camp,' she said, as she left the longhouse.

When I went outside, I counted nine tents in the clearing and five huts, not including the longhouse. The tents were only used for sleeping but the huts all seemed to have different uses. Apart from the toilet, there was a kitchen and a washing area. The other huts were used for storing things. One contained carpentry tools and another some boxes of tinned food.

As I wandered around the clearing, I found it strange that the camp was so deserted. Where was everybody? Where were my friends, Étienne and Françoise? I began to feel a little lonely and sorry for myself, so I decided to get out of the clearing and try to find them.

By good luck the path I chose led directly to the beach. I'd walked a few hundred metres when I noticed some people splashing around in the sea near one of the large rocks. At last I'd found someone. As I got nearer, I saw that there were six swimmers fishing with spears. They seemed to be catching a lot of fish. When they came out of the water onto the beach, none of the group noticed me. I had to stand there for a few moments, waiting for one of them to look up.

Étienne finally saw me. 'Richard! You are better!' He raced over to me. 'Everybody, this is our friend who was ill.'

'Hi, Richard,' the swimmers said.

23

I was introduced to all of them. Moshe, a tall Israeli guy with a loud laugh. Two Yugoslav girls whose names I could never pronounce and certainly never spell. And then Gregorio, who I liked at once. He had a kind face and a soft Latin accent.

As we walked back along the beach, Étienne told me about what I'd missed while I'd had a fever. Then Gregorio came up to me.

'You feel a bit strange with all these new people?'

'Oh, uh . . . yeah. A bit.'

'These first days are difficult, of course, but do not worry. You will find friends quickly, Richard.'

I smiled. The way he spoke made me feel a lot better.

When we got back to the camp, it was full of people. A fat guy was busy preparing fish outside the kitchen hut. Beside him a girl blew on a wood fire. Most of the people were just walking around the clearing, chatting. Gregorio was right. I did feel strange – a bit like a new boy in school. As I looked around, I wondered which of the faces would become my friends.

Chapter 4   Beach Life

After that first day, wandering around the clearing, I didn't really question a single thing about the beach.

I soon felt like I'd been living there all my life. Ko Samui became a dream-like place, and I couldn't remember anything about Bangkok. On the third or fourth day I remember thinking that Zeph and Sammy might arrive soon and wondering how people would react. Then I realized I couldn't quite remember what Zeph and Sammy looked like. A couple of days later, I'd forgotten they might be coming at all.

Routines developed quickly.

I'd wake up at about seven, seven-thirty, and go straight down to the beach for a swim with Étienne and another guy called Keaty. Then we'd go back to the camp and wash the sea salt off our bodies in the shower hut.

Breakfast was at eight. Every morning the people doing the cooking would boil a lot of rice and it was each individual's responsibility to cook anything else they wanted. Most people had their rice plain, but a few made the effort to boil some fish or vegetables. I never bothered.

After breakfast people would separate. Mornings were for working, and everybody had a job to do. By nine the camp was always empty. There were four main areas of work: fishing, gardening, cooking and carpentry.

Étienne, Françoise and I were in a fishing group. When we'd arrived there'd been two fishing groups, but we made it three. We were in one group with Gregorio. Moshe and the two Yugoslav girls were in another, and the last group was three Swedish guys called Karl, Sten and Christo. They were very serious about their fishing, and every day they'd swim through the caves in the cliff to the open sea.

I felt lucky to be working in the fishing group. If Étienne and Françoise hadn't volunteered to go fishing on the first day, we might have had to do gardening or cooking. Those jobs didn't appeal to me.

If there was a leader in the camp, it was Sal. When she talked, people listened. She spent her days walking around, checking that people were working properly. At first she spent a lot of time making sure we were settling in OK. After the first week she seemed satisfied and we rarely saw her during the work period.

The only person who didn't have a clear job was Jed. He spent his days alone and was usually the first person to leave in the mornings and the last person to come back. Keaty said that Jed spent a lot of time near the waterfall and above the cliffs. Sometimes he would disappear and spend the night somewhere on the island. When he came back he usually had some fresh dope, obviously taken from the dope fields.

At about two-thirty, people would start coming back to camp. The cooks and fishers would always be first so they could start preparing the fish. Then the gardeners would arrive with their vegetables and fruit, and by three the clearing would be full again.

Breakfast and dinner were the only meals of the day. Dinner was at four o'clock and people usually went to bed about nine. There wasn't much to do after dark, apart from getting stoned. Night-time camp fires weren't allowed because low planes could see them, even through the leafy ceiling.

Except for the people with tents, everybody slept in the longhouse. It took me a while to get used to sleeping with twenty-one other people, but soon I started enjoying it. There was a strong sense of closeness in the longhouse. Often, just as people were going to sleep, a voice from somewhere in the darkness would say, "Night Frankie." Then there'd be a short pause while we waited for someone else to say, 'Night, Sal,' or Gregorio, or Bugs, or anyone they felt like saying good night to. Then the named person would have to say good night to someone different, and it would go around the whole longhouse until everyone had been mentioned. No one's name was ever forgotten.

◆

On the morning of my fourth Sunday, everyone from the camp was down on the beach. Nobody worked on Sundays. The tide was out, so there was a large area of sand between the trees and the sea. Sal had organized a huge game of football. Nearly everyone was playing but not me and Keaty. We were sitting on a rock, chatting.

After a while I stood up. 'Feel like a swim?' I asked.

'Sure.'

'We could swim over to the coral. I haven't seen it yet.'

I swam down to the seabed and sat on the sand. Then I rested some stones on my lap so I wouldn't float back up again. Through my mask I could see the brightly coloured coral all around me in the hot tropical waters.

I looked up and saw Keaty's legs above me. He was sitting on a rock, and had attracted the attention of a little blue fish. It was mainly interested in biting his ankles. I rolled the stones off my lap and let myself float up to the surface. I pinched Keaty's ankle as I passed, using my fingernails like a row of teeth.

'Ow! What did you do that for?' said Keaty.

'There was this little fish . . .' I laughed.

'I thought it was a shark.'

'There are sharks here?' I asked in surprise.

'Millions.' He pointed out to the open sea.

I pulled myself out of the water and sat next to Keaty on the rock. He started rolling a joint.

'How long have you been here?' I said.

27

'Two years. I met Sal in Chiang Mai and we got friendly. We travelled around Thailand a bit together, then she told me about this place and brought me here.'

'Tell me about Mr Duck. Daffy. No one talks about him.'

'Yeah. People were shocked when they heard he'd died,' Keaty said. 'I didn't really know him. He was a bit distant, to me anyway. I mean, I knew who he was, but we didn't talk much.'

'So who was he?'

Keaty looked surprised. 'You don't know anything, do you, Rich? Haven't you seen the tree yet? The tree by the waterfall? You've been here just over a month!'

'Um, I don't think so.'

'Man!' Keaty smiled. 'I'll take you there tomorrow. Then you'll see.'

'OK,' I said, as he disappeared underwater.

That night, just as the light was starting to fade, we were given our sea-shell necklaces. Sal and her boyfriend, Bugs, wandered over to where we were sitting and gave them to us. The necklaces were important to me. However friendly everyone was, Étienne, Françoise and I were the only ones without them. Now we'd got them, I felt we'd been officially accepted.

I slipped the necklace over my head. 'Well, thanks a lot, Sal.'

'Thank Bugs. He made yours.'

'OK. Thanks, Bugs. It's a really nice necklace.'

He nodded, then began walking back to the longhouse. I couldn't make up my mind about Bugs. It was weird, because he was exactly the kind of guy I usually make friends with. But there was something about him that I didn't like.

◆

My suntan was progressing well. The sky had been mainly cloudy over the first few days, but now I was getting as brown as I'd ever been.

'Cool,' I said the next day when we were fishing, noticing how dark my skin was.

Étienne looked round. 'What is it?'

'Just my suntan. I'm getting really brown.'

Étienne nodded. 'I thought maybe you were thinking of this place.'

'The beach?'

'You said "Cool," so I thought you were thinking how good it is here.'

'Oh, well, I often think that … I mean, it was worth the trouble, wasn't it? After that long swim, and the dope fields. You fish, swim, eat, lie around, and everyone's so friendly. It's such a simple life. If I could stop the world and restart life, put the clock back, I think I'd restart it like this. For everyone. You know what I mean?'

Étienne nodded. 'All these thoughts are the same as mine. The same as everybody's.'

I got out of the water and checked my watch. It was exactly midday. 'I think I'll go and find Keaty now. He's going to show me a tree.'

'Tree?'

'A tree by the waterfall. Tell the others where I've gone. See you later.'

Since arriving at the beach, I'd only been to the waterfall a couple of times, and never on my own. It was partly because I had no reason to go there but also, I now understood, because the area made me feel nervous. It represented a link between the beach and the outside world, the world I'd nearly forgotten.

I found Keaty near the vegetable garden where he worked.

'Hey,' he said when he saw me. 'What are you doing here?'

'You were going to show me a tree. I left work early.'

'Right. I forgot. Let's go.'

It was a tree about twenty metres high to the right of the

29

pool. I'd noticed it before when I'd been wondering how to get down from the top of the waterfall. Keaty showed me the marks cut into one side of the trunk. Three names and four numbers. Bugs, Sylvester and Daffy. The numbers were all zeros.

Sylvester? Another name from a children's film, like Bugs Bunny and Daffy Duck. 'Who's Sylvester in the camp?' I asked Keaty.

'*Salvester.*'

'Oh, so Sylvester is Sal, right?'

He nodded.

'So they were the first people here?'

'The first. Nineteen eighty-nine. The three of them hired a boat from Ko Pha-Ngan.'

'They knew about this place already, or ...'

'Depends who you talk to. Bugs said he'd heard about a hidden lagoon from some fishermen on Ko Phalui but Daffy used to say they found the place by chance.'

'By chance?'

'Yeah, that's what he said. They didn't start the camp until nineteen-ninety. They spent the second half of eighty-nine going round India, then came back to Ko Pha-Ngan at the end of the year. They saw that Ko Pha-Ngan was becoming as spoilt as Ko Samui. And they wanted to stay somewhere completely unspoilt. Especially Daffy. They really knew what they were doing. They'd organized most things in the camp by the time Sal brought me here which was ... uh ... ninety-three.'

'So when you came, were there as many people as now?'

'More or less. Apart from the Swedes and Jed.'

I looked back at the tree. 'And the zeros. What do they mean?'

Keaty smiled. 'That was Daffy's idea. It's a date.'

'A date? The date of what?'

'The date they first arrived.'

'I thought that was eighty-nine.'

30

'It was.' Keaty touched the tree. 'But Daffy used to call it year zero.'

We started walking back towards the camp and I thought about what Keaty had told me. The more I thought about it, the more I liked the idea of what Sal, Bugs and Daffy had done. From Keaty's words I pictured the scene. January nineteen-ninety, maybe New Year's Eve, Ko Pha-Ngan. Daffy, Bugs and Sal talking as the sun starts coming up. Sal's found a boat to hire, Bugs has some tools in his backpack, Daffy's got a sack of rice and perhaps some bars of chocolate. By seven that morning they're walking down the beach. They don't look back, they just get into their boat and sail for the hidden paradise they'd found a year before. I found myself wishing I could meet Mr Duck again. I wanted to shake him by the hand.

As we passed the kitchen hut, Keaty and I looked in to say hello to the guy who was the main cook. His face was an angry red and shining with sweat.

'What's wrong?' I asked.

'The rice,' he said, marching out of the kitchen hut to one of the huts used for storing food.

We followed behind. 'There!' he said, pointing to three empty sacks and two full ones.

'What's the problem?' said Keaty.

The guy tore open the top of the nearest full sack and rice poured out; black and green, completely rotten.

I covered my nose and mouth to block the terrible smell. 'Ugh! That's horrible!'

The guy pointed up to the roof.

'It leaked?' I asked.

He nodded, too angry to speak, then marched back to his cooking.

'Well,' said Keaty, as we walked back to his tent. 'It isn't all bad news about the rice. You should be glad, Rich.'

'Why?'

'No more rice means a Rice Run. You can get some more cigarettes.'

In the tent, Keaty lay on his back, smoking one of my last cigarettes.

'I think,' he said, 'there are two main reasons why people don't like doing the Rice Run. Number one, it's a complete nuisance. Number two, it means visiting the World.'

'The World?' I asked.

'The World. It's another Daffy thing. The World is everything outside the beach.'

'So what happens on the Rice Run?'

'A couple of people take the boat and go to Ko Pha-Ngan. Then they buy some rice and come back here.'

'We've got a boat?' I asked.

'Of course. Not all of us are such good swimmers as you, Rich.'

'I didn't realize ... I didn't think about that ... Well, a quick trip to Ko Pha-Ngan doesn't sound too bad.'

'Yeah.' Now Keaty was grinning. 'But you haven't seen the boat yet.'

An hour later, the entire camp sat in a circle. The news about the rice had been passed around quickly, and Sal had called a meeting.

Keaty was sitting next to me. 'I bet Jed volunteers,' he whispered. 'He loves doing special duties.'

I was going to reply when Sal clapped her hands and stood up. 'OK,' she said. 'As everyone knows we've got a problem. We thought we had another seven weeks of rice but we've only got enough for two days. Now, this isn't a major crisis, nobody's going to starve to death, but it is a minor one.' Sal paused. 'Well, you know what I'm going to say next. We need to go on a Rice Run. So ... who's volunteering?'

Jed put up his hand immediately.

'What did I tell you?' whispered Keaty.

'Thank you, Jed. So OK ... that's one ... Who else?' Sal looked around. Most people were looking at the ground. 'Come on ... We all know Jed can't do it alone ...'

Just as when I jumped from the waterfall, I only realized what I was doing after I'd started doing it. I put my hand up.

Sal noticed, then glanced at Bugs. Out of the corner of my eye I saw him nod.

'Are you volunteering too, Richard?'

'Yeah,' I answered, still a little surprised to find that I was. 'I mean ... yeah. I'm volunteering.'

Sal smiled. 'Good. That's decided then. You'll leave tomorrow morning.'

There wasn't much preparation to be done. All we needed was money and the clothes on our backs, and Sal produced the money. I spent the rest of the afternoon trying to explain to Keaty, Étienne and Françoise why I'd volunteered.

'I hope you are not bored with life here,' Françoise said, as we chatted outside the longhouse entrance.

I laughed. 'No, I just thought it might be interesting. Anyway, I haven't seen Ko Pha-Ngan yet.'

'Good. It would be sad to be bored with paradise, no? If you are bored with paradise, what is left?'

Chapter 5   The Rice Run

Jed wouldn't let me wake Étienne and Françoise the next morning. They'd asked me to say goodbye before I left but Jed shook his head and said, 'Unnecessary.'

I thought his knife was unnecessary too. He got it out as we stood on the beach, preparing for the swim to the cliffs. A green-handled knife with a sharp blade.

'What's that for?' I asked.

'It's just a tool,' he replied. Then he grinned and added, 'Frightening, huh?' before going into the water with the knife between his teeth.

Until the Rice Run, Jed was a mystery to me. After the first day, when he'd met us at the waterfall, we'd had almost no contact with him. Sometimes I saw him in the evenings – never earlier, because he returned to the camp so late – but we'd never really had a good conversation. Normally I make quick judgements about people, often completely wrong, but with Jed I'd kept an open mind.

When we got to the cliffs, Jed explained that there were three caves that led into the open sea and our boat. We had to swim through one of them.

'You know this cave?' Jed asked, when we got to the entrance.

'I've seen it while I've been fishing.'

'But you've never swum through it?'

'No.'

He looked concerned. 'You should have. Golden rule: first thing you do when you arrive somewhere is find out how you can get out again. These caves are the only way out of the lagoon.'

You couldn't see through to the open sea, because the roof of

34

the cave dropped below water-level. Jed explained that we had to swim through an underwater passage in the cave. I wasn't happy about swimming into the blackness, but Jed assured me that it was easy. 'You don't have to swim underwater for long. You get to the sea before you know it.'

'Really?'

'Yeah. It's low tide so we only have to swim underwater through half the cave. When it's high tide you have to swim like that through the whole cave and even that's easy.' Then he took a deep breath and slipped underwater, leaving me alone.

I waited a minute in the water just inside the cave, listening to my splashes echo round the walls. My feet and legs were cold, reminding me of the diving game with Étienne and Françoise off Ko Samui. The echo began to scare me so much that I dived down into the inky water of the cave.

Unusually for me, I kept my eyes shut as I swam. I guessed that with each kick I swam about a metre, and carefully counted my strokes to give me a sense of distance. After I'd counted ten, I began to feel worried. An ache was building up in my lungs, and Jed had said that the underwater passage was no more than a forty-second swim. At fifteen strokes I realized I had to make a decision about whether to turn back. I gave myself a limit of three more kicks, then my fingertips suddenly broke the surface of the water.

I knew something was wrong as soon as I took a breath. The air was so bad that, even though I needed oxygen desperately, I could only manage short breaths before I started being sick. I looked around me, but it was so dark I couldn't even see my fingers in front of my face.

'Jed!' I called.

Not even an echo.

My first thought was that I should continue to swim down the passage. I assumed that I'd surfaced too soon, maybe into a pocket of air left open by the low tide. But I'd lost my sense of direction and didn't know which way to swim. By feeling around with my hands and feet I seemed to find four passages, but it was hard to judge. There could have been even more. It was a frightening discovery. If there'd only been two passages, then whichever direction I chose to swim in, I'd either come up in the lagoon again or the sea. But these other passages could lead to nowhere.

My second thought was to stay where I was and hope Jed would come to find me, but that wasn't very appealing either. I felt I'd go mad if I waited in the blackness.

For a minute I stayed still, thinking about what to do. Then I started to panic. I splashed around wildly, knocking into the walls, screaming out 'Help.' Then a second later, ignoring the disgusting smell, I breathed in deeply and went underwater. I took whichever of the four passages I found first and swam as hard as I could.

I felt terrible. My legs and hands were knocking painfully against the passage walls and there was a deep pain in my chest. After perhaps fifty seconds I began to see red through the darkness. 'It means I'm dying,' I told myself, as the colour grew brighter. In the middle of the redness a spot of light started to form — yellow, but I expected it to turn white. I was remembering a TV programme about how dying people see lights at the end of tunnels. Then, suddenly, I realized that the redness might not be death after all. It might be light, sunlight, passing through the water and the lids of my tightly shut eyes. I forced myself to make one more hard kick and came straight up into brightness and fresh air. There was Jed, sitting in the sun on a rock! Beside him was a long boat, painted the same blue-green as the sea.

'Hey,' he said, not looking round. 'You were a long time.'
I couldn't answer at first because I couldn't breathe properly.
'What were you doing back there?'

'Drowning,' I finally managed to say. 'Didn't you hear me?'

'Sure,' he said, running the blade of his knife against his beard. 'Now we've got to get the boat started.'

'Jed! Listen to me! I was stuck in an air pocket with more than one exit and nearly drowned!'

For the first time, Jed looked at me. 'An air pocket?' he said. 'Are you sure?'

'Of course I'm sure!'

Jed frowned. 'Well ... that's weird. I've been through there a hundred times and I've never found any air pockets. And there were several exits?'

'Four at least. I could feel them and I didn't know which one I should take. It was terrible.'

'I'm sorry, Richard, I really am. I honestly didn't know that could happen. It's amazing. Everybody on the beach has swum through that cave and no one's ever got lost.'

He held out a hand and pulled me on to the rock.

'I might have died.'

Jed nodded. 'You might have. I'm sorry.'

Twenty minutes later, I was ready to set off for Ko Pha-Ngan. I liked our boat immediately. I liked its South-East Asian shape and the brightly painted patterns on the front.

'Right,' I said, when we were both in the boat. 'Let's start the engine.' I recognized the engine type. 'Here we go!' I shouted, and the engine roared into life.

When we set off, I was keen to get to Ko Pha-Ngan. I was pleased to be doing something important for the beach. But an hour later, as the shape of the island was forming on the horizon, my keenness began to be replaced by anxiety. I was suddenly aware that meeting the World would bring back all the things I'd forgotten. I wasn't exactly sure what these things were, but I knew I didn't want to be reminded of them. I looked at Jed and guessed that he was feeling the same. To avoid thinking about the

37

World, I started day-dreaming about Françoise and how beautiful she was.

'West ... more ... land ...' I suddenly heard over the noise of the engine.

I stopped dreaming and shouted out, 'What?'

'I'm going west! There's more open beach to land on. Fewer beach huts.'

I nodded in agreement. While I'd been thinking about Françoise, Ko Pha-Ngan had got much closer. I could now see the trunks and leaves of some coconut trees, and the midday shadows beneath them.

The stretch of beach we landed on was empty apart from a few old beach huts. We jumped out of the boat and dragged it up on to the beach.

'Are we going to leave the boat here?' I asked.

'No, we'll have to hide it.' Jed pointed to the trees. 'Maybe up there. Go and make sure the area is completely empty.'

'OK.'

Not far from where we'd landed I found two trees with a bush between them. The bush would cover the boat completely and the nearest beach huts were fifty metres away.

'Here seems fine,' I called to Jed.

'Right. Come and help me then.'

With the weight of the engine, the boat was very heavy. Eventually we managed to get it between the trees and under the bush. We were both completely exhausted and looking forward to a drink and a big meal.

An hour later, we were walking past rows of busy beach huts and sunbathers. I was surprised that people weren't taking more notice of us. Everyone looked so strange to me that I couldn't believe I didn't look equally strange to them.

'Let's eat,' said Jed, and we walked into the nearest café and sat down. Jed looked at the menu while I looked around me in amazement. Even the plastic chair I was sitting on was strangely uncomfortable. I couldn't work out the right way to sit on it.

'How do you sit on these things?' I said.

Jed looked up and laughed. 'It's weird, isn't it? All this. After the camp.'

'Yeah, it certainly is.'

'What do you want to eat? I'm starving.'

I looked at the menu. 'I think I'd like a couple of hamburgers.'

After we'd eaten, Jed gave me a choice. I could go with him to buy the rice or I could stay on the beach and meet him later. He didn't really need my help so I decided to stay. I had my own shopping to do, anyway. I wanted to buy some more cigarettes and a few presents. I found a small shop and bought some razor blades for me, Étienne, Gregorio and Keaty, and a tube of toothpaste for Françoise. Then I bought several packets of sweets – I wanted to give everyone a present – and finally I bought myself some cigarettes and a pair of shorts.

I had a drink and decided to pass the time by walking along the beach. After a while the heat made me feel tired, and I lay down in the shade for an afternoon sleep.

The music started at eight, which was lucky or I might have slept until midnight. I jumped up and ran down the beach to the café. It was now full of people, but I saw Jed immediately. He had a bottle of beer in his hands and he was looking extremely annoyed.

'Where have you been?' he said angrily, when I sat down beside him. 'I've been waiting . . .'

'I'm sorry,' I replied. 'I fell asleep . . .'

He still looked very angry.

'What's the matter? Didn't you get the rice?'

'I got the rice, Richard. Don't worry about that.'

'What's wrong then?'

'*You* tell *me*.'

'Tell you ...?'

'About two Americans.'

'Two Americans?'

Jed drank his beer. 'Two Americans I heard talking about an idyllic beach in the marine park.'

'Oh God!'

'They know you, Richard. They used your name. And they've got a map.' He squeezed his eyes shut like he was fighting to keep control of his temper. 'A map, Richard! They were showing it to some Germans!'

I shook my head. I was feeling shocked. 'I'd forgotten ... I'd ...'

'Who are they?'

'Jed, wait. You don't understand. *I* didn't tell them about the beach. *They* told *me*. They already knew about it.'

He put his beer bottle down on the table hard. '*Who are they?*' he shouted.

'Zeph and Sammy. I met them on Ko Samui. They were just two guys in the hut next to mine. We spent some time together, and the evening before we were going to leave for Ko Phelong they started talking about the beach.'

'So you drew them a map?'

'No! I didn't say a thing, Jed. None of us did.'

'Then where did the map come from?'

'The next morning ... I drew it and pushed it under their door ...' I pulled out a cigarette and tried to light it. My hands trembled and it took me three attempts.

'Why?'

'I was worried. I didn't know if the beach really existed. I had to tell someone where we were going in case something went wrong.'

'What could go wrong?'

40

'I don't know! We didn't know anything! I just didn't want us disappearing with nobody knowing where we'd gone.'

Jed put his head in his hands. 'This could be bad.'

'We could have disappeared into the marine park and no one would have . . .'

He nodded slowly. 'I understand that.'

We sat in silence for several minutes. Eventually Jed said, 'These two Americans. Do you think they'll try to come to our island?'

'They might do, Jed. I don't know them well enough.'

'God! This could be *so* bad.' Then suddenly he laid his hand on my arm. 'Listen,' he said. 'Are you blaming yourself?'

I nodded.

'Don't. I'm serious. Whatever happens with these Americans, it isn't your fault. If I'd been in your situation, I'd have done the same thing.'

'What do you mean, "whatever happens"?' I asked.

'I mean . . . I mean whatever happens I don't want you to blame yourself. It's important, Richard. If you really want someone to blame, blame Daffy. Anyway, we might not even have a problem. In a few weeks the Americans will probably be flying home and the map should go with them. Even if they stay in Thailand they might not bother trying to reach us. The trip isn't easy.'

'Well, I hope you're right,' I said quietly.

'All we can do is hope . . . and wait.' He finished his beer and stood up. 'We've got to get the rice back to the boat now. Are you ready?'

'Yes.'

Around the back of the café was a narrow passage between two beach huts. Jed had hidden the rice sacks there. We set off along the beach, dragging the sacks along the sand.

After a while we stopped for a cigarette and ate some of the sweets I'd bought.

'I'm sorry if I was angry with you,' Jed said. 'You didn't deserve it.'

'It's all right.'

'When we get back to the camp, Richard, don't mention the Americans to anyone.'

'But . . .'

'Sal and Bugs. I don't think they'll understand.'

'OK. If you think that's the right thing to do.'

It took us another three hours to get back to the boat. We left the sacks beside it, then lay down on the sand. Jed went to sleep at once. I lay beside him and looked up at the stars, wishing I was living in a world where I hadn't given the map to Zeph and Sammy.

♦

We woke up at dawn the next day, put the rice in the boat, and made the journey back to our island. When we got back to the camp, no one seemed at all interested in our trip. A few asked 'How was it?' out of politeness, but as soon as I began telling them they looked bored. And no one was very enthusiastic about the presents I'd bought them either. It seemed that they weren't interested in anything outside the beach.

I was disappointed by their reactions, but not for long. I soon began to forget the World too, as I had when we first arrived at the camp. Within a week nothing much existed for me beyond the lagoon and its circle of cliffs.

My worries about Zeph and Sammy didn't disappear so quickly, though. I was kept awake, worrying about what plans they and the mysterious Germans might be making. But it was hard to go on worrying, even about them, as the days passed and nothing happened.

♦

A few weeks after the Rice Run I woke up to the noise of rain on the longhouse roof. It had rained only three or four times since I'd arrived at the beach, and no more than short showers. This was a tropical storm, even heavier than the one on Ko Samui.

A few of us stood around the longhouse entrance, looking out across the clearing. Bugs was standing outside in the pouring rain, looking up at the sky.

'Stupid fool,' someone said, looking at Bugs.

'Thinks he's God,' someone else said, and we all laughed. I would have said something too, but just then Sal came out of the far end of the longhouse and started walking towards us.

'What's the delay?' she asked.

Nobody answered her so I said, 'Delay about what?'

She looked at me and said angrily. 'Fishing, gardening – work. What are we going to eat with your rice if no one goes fishing or gardening?'

People started slowly moving out into the rain. As I ran down to the beach, I thought about the conversation at the longhouse entrance. I'd never mentioned the way Bugs annoyed me, not even to Keaty. But from the way the others were talking, I began to wonder if they felt the same way. The thing that I'd noticed most was the way we'd all gone quiet when Sal came over. I felt like I'd witnessed some kind of division among the people in the camp, and possibly been included in it.

◆

The rain continued to pour all that week and half the next, but in the early hours of Thursday morning it stopped. Everyone was relieved.

One day, on my way back from the beach where we'd been fishing, I met Sal.

'Richard, are you going back to the camp?'

'Yes.'

'Will you walk with me to the garden? I've got to go down there and I'd like some company. We haven't had a good chat for a long time.'

I nodded. 'OK, sure.'

Sal walked slowly. Sometimes she paused to look at flowers, sometimes she stopped for no apparent reason.

'Richard,' she said after some time, 'I want to tell you how pleased we all are that you found our secret beach.'

'Thanks, Sal,' I replied, already understanding that this conversation wasn't just a friendly chat.

'Can I be frank, Richard? When you three arrived, we were all a little worried. Perhaps you can understand why . . .'

'Of course.'

'But you all fitted in so *well*. Better than we could have hoped. We really appreciated you doing the Rice Run, Richard.'

'Oh, well,' I said, trying to look modest.

'I feel a little guilty about the way I spoke to you that miserable wet morning at the longhouse entrance. I don't consider myself to be the leader here, but . . .'

'You are the leader really, Sal.'

'Oh, maybe in some ways I am.' She laughed. 'People come to me with their problems and I try to sort them out. Keaty, for example. I know you and Keaty are close, so I presume you know about his problem.'

'He wants to stop gardening.' I knew Keaty hated work in the garden and wanted to join one of the fishing groups.

'That's right. But it isn't easy moving people to different jobs. I've been telling him it isn't possible for months. He was going to start fishing when your little group arrived. He was terribly disappointed, Richard. I realize now that if I'm going to improve his situation, I'm going to have to move someone.'

'Who?' I asked in an anxious voice.

44

'I'm sorry, Richard, but it has to be you. I don't have a choice.'

'Oh no, Sal. Please, I really don't want to move. I love fishing and I'm good at it.'

'I *know* you are, Richard, I *know*. But try to see it from my position. Keaty needs to move out of the garden, I can't separate Étienne and Françoise or the three Swedes. Gregorio has been fishing for two years, the Yugoslavs don't know how to do anything else. Honestly, Richard, if I had a choice ...'

'Yeah,' I said, looking at the ground.

'And I'm not going to make you do gardening.'

'You aren't?' A terrible thought crossed my mind. If I wasn't going to do gardening, maybe I'd be doing carpentry with Bugs. Any job would be better than that.

'No, you'll be working with Jed. He wants a partner on his trips round the island and he suggested you.'

I looked up. 'Jed? Cool!' It had never occurred to me that Jed might want someone with him. Although we'd become friendly, I thought he preferred being alone.

'I know,' Sal continued, apparently reading my mind. 'I was surprised too. You must have made a good impression on the Rice Run.'

'But what does Jed need help with? Doesn't he just ... steal dope?'

'He does that, yes, but other things as well. He'll explain.'

'I see.'

Sal smiled. 'Richard, I'm so glad we've sorted all this out. I've been worried about telling you for days. Now we can go and find Keaty. Would you like to give him the good news or shall I?'

We walked to the garden together. When we got there, Keaty had already left for the camp so I ran after him.

'I feel terrible about this, Richard,' he said, when I'd told him the news. 'I didn't want Sal to move you out of the fishing group.'

'No, it isn't your fault. It's just bad luck.'

We walked in silence for a few moments, then Keaty said, 'Do you know why Jed's suddenly decided he needs help?'

'I don't even know what he needs help with. We still don't know what he does in the jungle.'

When we got nearer the clearing, it seemed to me that people must have heard the news. They paused in their conversations and all turned, watching me with quiet and serious looks on their faces. There was a strange moment when I reached them. I felt like I'd already been isolated from them. It reminded me of the first morning, after my fever, when I discovered that Étienne and Françoise had made friends while I'd been asleep.

It took me over two hours to get to sleep that night. For the first time since arriving on the beach, I started thinking about home. Almost wishing I could return, in fact. Not to leave the beach permanently – just to contact a few important people and let them know I was still alive and OK. My family in particular, and a few of my friends.

Chapter 6   Disaster Strikes

Jed's eyes were a little wider apart than mine, so I had to adjust the binoculars before I could see clearly. It took me several seconds to find the beach on the island next to ours, but then I saw the five familiar figures almost immediately. They were in the same place they'd been yesterday morning and nearly every morning for the past nine days, except for four days ago when the beach had been completely deserted. That had caused us a bit of concern until they reappeared from the trees a couple of hours later.

'They're still there,' I said.

'What are they doing?' asked Jed.

'Just lying there.'

'And you can count all five?'

I paused. 'Five, yeah. They're all there.'

'Good.' Jed coughed quietly into his hand. We had to be careful about noise, so close to the dope fields. We couldn't smoke either, which didn't help my nerves. 'Good.'

◆

My first day with Jed had started badly. I'd woken up in a terrible mood, still thinking about my family and friends in England. I was also rather depressed about not going fishing with the others. But as soon as he'd explained about the people he'd seen on the neighbouring island, I'd understood.

Then I'd started panicking, saying, 'This is the worst thing that could happen,' again and again, while Jed waited patiently for me to calm down. It took some time, but eventually I stopped talking for long enough for him to speak, and he was able to explain the situation to me.

47

The good news was that Sal didn't know that I'd given Zeph and Sammy the map of our island. After Jed had seen five people on the island next to ours – the island Étienne, Françoise and I had swum from to reach our beach island – he'd only told Sal that some strangers had arrived there. He didn't mention their connection with me. She thought that Jed had asked for a partner because he'd got tired of working alone. The other good news was that the people hadn't moved from the island. If they were aiming for our beach, they were obviously finding it difficult to reach us.

However, we had to assume that they did want to get to our beach eventually. We also had to assume that two of them were Zeph and Sammy, and the other three were the Germans that Jed had seen on Ko Pha-Ngan when we did the Rice Run. We couldn't be sure about this because the people were too small to see clearly through Jed's binoculars, but it seemed likely.

When Jed had told me the bad news, I'd spent the rest of that day in a state of shock, watching the five people through his binoculars. Every time one of them appeared to move, I was sure that they were going to start swimming towards us. But they didn't. In fact, they hardly moved from their patch of sand, occasionally going into the sea for a few minutes or disappearing into the jungle behind the beach for a couple of hours.

After three or four similar days had passed, my initial level of panic faded and I just felt generally tense. With the tension I was able to think more clearly. That was when I began to notice other things about my new job with Jed.

The first was getting to know Jed more. We spent every hour until nightfall sitting on a rock at the highest point of our island. Apart from spying, all we could do was talk. Mostly we talked about Plan B, which was what we were going to do when the five people finally got here. The only problem with Plan B was that, like most Plan Bs, it didn't exist. We had several options, but we could never agree on which one was the best. The option I favoured was that Jed went down to meet them and told then that they weren't welcome, but he didn't want to do that. Although he was sure he'd be able to make them leave, he was also sure that they'd go straight back to Ko Pha-Ngan and tell everyone what they'd found. Instead, Jed wanted to rely on our island's natural barriers. There was the long swim from the island, then they had to get past the dope guards, find the lagoon, and then find a way of getting down the waterfall. Jed was confident that this would all be too difficult for them. I didn't like to remind him that Étienne, Françoise and I had managed it. It was during one of our endless Plan B discussions that Jed told me about the main aim of his job – to look out for new people who were trying to find our beach.

◆

'Something's bothering me,' I said, putting down the binoculars.

Jed frowned. 'What?'

'I'm afraid they'll find our backpacks. We couldn't swim with them so we hid them under some bushes. If Zeph and Sammy find them, they'll know we were there and that they're near our beach.'

'How well did you hide them?'

'Quite well. I'm starting to think that I might have copied the map wrong. I drew it in a real hurry and I could have missed out an island between Ko Phelong and here.'

Jed nodded. 'It's possible.'

'So if they think they're on *our* island now, that explains why they haven't moved for the last nine days. They're looking for our beach ... which they won't find ... but they might find the backpacks.'

'It's possible,' Jed repeated. 'But they sit in the same place all day. It faces us, right? So they *know* this is the right island. They're sitting there and trying to work out how to reach us ...'

We looked at each other briefly, then I started staring through the binoculars again.

Jed and I would stay on the rock until the sun set, then we'd go back to the camp. We couldn't spy if it was too dark to see, and anyway, Jed said it wasn't safe to be outside the camp after nightfall. You didn't know what or who you might meet. Back at camp, Jed would go and talk to Sal and I'd get some dinner. Then I'd go and look for Étienne, Françoise and Keaty. Usually I'd find them near the kitchen hut, having a joint before bedtime.

Lying to Sal about Zeph and Sammy and the map was easy, but I hated lying to my friends. However, I didn't have a choice. Until we knew whether Zeph and Sammy would manage to get to our beach, there was no sense in worrying everyone. I could only tell them that my new job involved looking out for people who might be trying to find our beach.

'It's a good idea,' said Keaty. 'What will you do if you see someone coming?'

'I'll tell you when it happens,' I replied, laughing uncomfortably.

♦

At the end of the tenth day working with Jed we were, as usual, hurrying to get back to the camp before nightfall.

My plan was to eat some food quickly and then spend the rest of the evening with my friends. But when I got to the kitchen hut, all I found was a cold pile of boiled rice. The cooking pots for fish and vegetables were empty. Then I noticed something even more strange. Apart from Jed, the clearing seemed to be completely deserted.

I walked over to Jed. 'Do you notice anything weird?' I said.

'Well, I can't see any food.'

'Exactly. There isn't any food. And there aren't any people either.'

Jed stood up and shone his torch around him. 'Yeah,' he said. 'That *is* weird . . .'

We looked around us for a few seconds, our eyes following the light from the torch. Then, from somewhere nearby, there was a loud moan, the sound of someone in a lot of pain.

'God, did you hear that?' whispered Jed.

We paused, listening carefully. Then we heard the moan again, and the hairs on the back of my neck stood up. There was something frightening about the empty camp in the darkness.

'OK,' said Jed, 'we'd better investigate.'

We'd only walked a little way when someone put their head out of one of the tents. It was a girl called Ella.

'Jed? Richard?'

'Yeah, it's us. What's going on, Ella?'

She shook her head. 'Come inside. It's a disaster.'

We went in. One of the cooks was lying inside the tent. His eyes were closed and he was holding his stomach.

'It was Keaty. Stupid fool,' Ella said, wiping the sweat from the guy's forehead.

'Keaty? Why? What did he do?' I asked.

'He put a squid in one of the fishing buckets, and we cut it up and cooked it with everything else.'

'So?'

'The squid was already dead when he speared it. Most of the people in the camp have food poisoning and are being violently sick. Only five or six of us are all right. I've got a bit of a stomach ache but I think I've been lucky.'

'And why did Keaty spear a dead squid?'

'I'd like to ask him that myself. We'd all like to ask him,' said Ella in an angry voice.

'Where is he?' I asked. 'In his tent?

'Maybe.'

'OK. Well, I'll go and talk to him.'

It took me ages to find Keaty. He wasn't in his tent, and there was no response in the clearing when I called his name. Eventually I decided to check the beach, where I saw him, sitting in a patch of moonlight a little way down the shore.

'Hi,' he said in a low voice.

I nodded and sat beside him.

'I'm not very popular at the moment, Rich.'

'Neither is squid!'

He didn't laugh.

'So what happened?' I asked.

'Don't you know? I poisoned the camp.'

'Yeah, but . . .'

'I was fishing, using Gregorio's mask. I saw this squid, we've eaten squid a hundred times before, so I speared it and threw it in the bucket. I didn't know it was already dead.'

'But if it wasn't moving . . .'

'Yeah, well I know that now! But I thought . . . I thought its arms were moving . . .'

'So it was a mistake. It wasn't your fault.'

'God, Rich! Of course it was my fault!' he shouted, and looked away.

I only stayed with Keaty for a few minutes because I wanted to find Étienne and Françoise. He wouldn't come with me because he said he wasn't ready to face people yet, the poor guy.

When I saw what was happening inside the longhouse, I was glad Keaty had decided to stay on the beach. The scene inside would only have made him feel worse. I'd had no idea that the effects of food poisoning had been so severe. Everybody was moaning and there was a strong sour smell throughout the longhouse. People were crying out for water or for the vomit to be wiped off their chests.

I eventually found Françoise and Étienne. Étienne was asleep, so I suppose he might have been unconscious, but he was

52

breathing steadily and his forehead didn't feel too hot. Françoise, however, was awake and in a great deal of pain. She didn't cry out like everyone else but she bit her bottom lip, and all over her stomach were marks from where she'd been digging in her fingernails.

'Stop doing that,' I said firmly.

She looked at me through dull eyes. 'Richard?'

'Yes. Stop biting your lip.'

'What is happening, Richard?'

'You've got food poisoning.'

'I mean, what is happening to everyone else?'

'Well ...' I looked down the longhouse. I wasn't sure how to answer in case I frightened her. 'People are being sick ...'

'Do you think this is serious for us?'

'No, no,' I replied, laughing encouragingly. 'You'll all be much better tomorrow. You'll be fine.'

'Good ... Richard, I need some water ... Please will you bring me some?'

'Of course. I'll be back in two minutes.'

Outside I found Jed sitting in front of the kitchen hut, eating some plain rice. He held out his bowl as I approached and said, 'You should eat.'

'I'm not hungry. Have you seen inside the longhouse?'

He swallowed. 'I put my head round the door. The same thing's happening in the tents.'

'Are you worried?'

'Sure. People can die from food poisoning like this. We need to make them drink lots of water. And we need to keep ourselves fit so we can look after them. That's why you should eat something. You haven't eaten since morning.'

'Later,' I said, thinking of Françoise. I got some water and walked back to the longhouse.

While I'd been away, Françoise's condition had got worse. I

53

helped her drink the water and stayed with her until her breathing became slower and heavier and she finally fell asleep.

I don't really feel I have to explain what happened next, but I will anyway. I bent over and gave Françoise a kiss on the cheek. I remember noticing how soft and smooth her skin was. In the middle of that terrible night, with everyone moaning and all the vomit, I wasn't expecting to find sweetness. It took me a little by surprise and I closed my eyes for a few moments, just for the chance to forget about all the bad things that were happening. But when I looked up, Étienne was staring at me.

'What were you doing?' he asked.

'Nothing.'

'You were kissing Françoise!'

'So? I gave her a kiss on the cheek. You've seen me do that before.'

'You've never kissed her like that before. For so long!'

I felt exhausted. 'You've got this wrong,' I said. 'You're very ill. It's affecting you.'

Étienne didn't say anything.

I tried a joke. 'If I give *you* a kiss, will that make everything OK?'

He paused a bit longer, and finally nodded. 'I am sorry, Richard. You are right. I am ill and it is affecting me. But I can look after her now. Maybe some others need your help.'

'Yeah, I'm sure they do. Shout if you need anything.'

I stood up and glanced at Françoise, who was still fast asleep. Then I walked out of the longhouse.

That night I slept in the clearing. The last thing I remember before falling asleep was Sal's voice. She'd recovered enough to walk around, and was calling Keaty's name. I could have told her he was down on the beach, but I decided not to. I didn't like the sound of her voice. It was like a parent calling to a naughty kid.

◆

Jed woke me at about six-thirty with a bowl of rice. While I ate, he talked.

'Listen. One of us has to go and see what Zeph and Sammy are doing.'

'Oh, OK . . . But why not both of us?'

'Why do you think? Someone has to stay here to look after all these sick people – and I think it should be me. I know a little bit about first aid.'

'And what should I do if Zeph and Sammy are on their way here?'

Jed paused. 'I'm trying not think about it, but if they are then get back here as fast as you can and tell me. But before you go I want you to find Keaty and the Swedes. There are about fifteen people here who are well enough to eat, so someone's going to have to go fishing for them. Only the three Swedes and Keaty are healthy enough.'

I went down to the beach first and found Keaty sleeping in the same place. I assumed he'd had a bad night so I decided to smoke a cigarette before waking him up. I was just finishing it when Karl, Sten and Christo – the Swedes – appeared. I put my finger to my lips, pointing at Keaty, and we walked away from him so that he didn't wake up.

'You're going to be busy today,' I said to them.

Sten nodded. 'But there is only half the camp to fish for, no? We only need to catch fifteen fishes. Not so difficult, I think. Would you like to fish with us?'

'Thanks, but Keaty will wake up soon.'

'Ah yes, Keaty. Is he sick?'

'No, he's fine. A bit depressed, but he didn't get food poisoning.'

'That is good. Well, we should be going. We will see you later, Richard.'

'OK.'

Sten said something to Karl and Christo in Swedish. Then they walked down to the shore and began swimming towards the caves.

When I got back to Keaty, he was awake.

'Hi,' I said. 'Did you sleep all right?'

He shook his head. 'Are things bad at the camp?'

'They were last night. It's better now but people are still being sick.'

Keaty sat up and rubbed the sand off his legs and arms. 'I should get back. Got to help.'

'No, don't go back yet. They want you to do some fishing.'

'They want *me* to go fishing? After the squid!'

'That's what Jed said. The Swedes will be fishing too, and most people won't be eating. Just catch a few fish.'

'OK then. See you later, Richard,' Keaty said, and set off down the beach towards the water.

Hours later, I made my way back to the camp after spending the afternoon watching Zeph, Sammy and the Germans through Jed's binoculars. The clearing was empty apart from Ella, who was cleaning a few fish outside the kitchen hut.

'I was hoping you'd bring some more fish,' she said when she saw me. 'Keaty's the only person who's brought me any.'

'What about the Swedes? Haven't they come back yet?'

'No they haven't. What time is it anyway?'

I looked at my watch. 'Six-thirty. I wonder why they're taking so long. Maybe it's the boat – perhaps the engine broke down or they ran out of petrol.'

Ella looked annoyed. 'Maybe,' she said. 'But if you think about it, they could have swum back by now.'

I thought about this last comment of Ella's as I walked towards the longhouse, because she was absolutely right. The Swedes could easily have swum back in two hours, even dragging the boat behind them.

56

In a way, then, I was already aware that something serious had happened to Sten, Karl and Christo. Logically, it was the only explanation. But there were too many problems in the camp to start worrying about new ones. As I entered the longhouse, people were calling out for water or for someone to clean up their vomit. I ran around helping people and didn't have time to think about the Swedes again for ages.

At a quarter to nine the longhouse door banged open.

'Oh there you are,' I started to say, but the words dried up in my throat.

Karl was half bent over and the expression on his face told us at once that there was something badly wrong. He took a single heavy step towards us, moving into the brighter candlelight. That was when we realized that he was carrying someone on his back – Sten. Suddenly Karl fell forwards without making any effort to stop himself, and Sten slipped off his back on to the floor. He was terribly injured – there was a circle of flesh as large as a football missing from his side.

Étienne was the first to move. He raced past me, almost knocking me to the ground. When I looked up, he was bending over Sten. I heard Sal behind me calling out, 'What's happened?', and then Karl began screaming at the top of his voice. For a minute people covered their ears as his cries filled the longhouse. It was only after Keaty had grabbed him, shouting at him to shut up, that he managed to say one word: 'Shark.'

The shocked silence after Karl said 'shark' only lasted a heartbeat. Then we all started talking again. A circle quickly formed around Karl and Sten – the same kind of circle you get in a school playground when people are fighting – and everyone started shouting out questions and making suggestions. Everyone wanted to be involved in the crisis. 'They need water!' and 'Put him in the recovery position!' and 'Hold his nose!'

I thought all the advice was stupid. You could see the air

bubbling out of the hole in Sten's side, so his lungs were obviously completely destroyed. And anyway, you couldn't imagine anyone looking more dead. His eyes were open but you could only see the whites. Karl could hardly be put in the recovery position while he was rolling around and screaming. The only person who was talking sense was Sal. She was shouting at everyone to get back and shut up. No one took any notice though.

I pushed my way backwards through the crowd, which was easy as most people were trying to get closer to the Swedes. As soon as I was out of the circle, I began thinking a lot more clearly. Two realizations hit me at once. Number one was that I now had a chance to have a cigarette. Number two was Christo. Nobody had even mentioned the third Swede, who might have been on the beach, wounded and waiting for help to arrive.

I hesitated for a couple of moments, then I made my decision and ran down the longhouse, passing the few squid-sufferers who were still too ill to see what was going on. Just before I ran out of the door, I lit a cigarette and shouted 'Christo!', but I didn't wait to see if anyone had heard me.

Through the jungle, I cursed myself for not having grabbed a torch. I couldn't see much apart from the red light from my cigarette. On the beach, however, there was enough moonlight to see clearly. Across the sand were deep tracks where Karl had dragged Sten. He seemed to have reached the beach about twenty metres from the path that led to the clearing. Christo, I noted, couldn't have reached the shore. In the light from the moon, the sand was silver. If he'd been there, I'd have seen him.

I took a deep breath and sat down near the water, wondering what to do. Christo wasn't on the beach, and I hadn't passed him on the path from the camp – unless I'd walked over him without realizing it – so he was in the lagoon, the open sea, or the cave that led to the sea. If he was in the open sea, he was probably dead. If he was in the lagoon, he was either on a rock or floating face down. If he was in the cave, he would be at one of its two entrances, maybe too tired or injured to swim through the underwater passage. The shark could be anywhere.

'I bet he's in the cave,' I said, and lit another cigarette to help me think.

When I reached the cave, I swam to the place where the passage went below the water level. Then I took a lungful of air and dived underwater. Every few strokes I stopped and felt around to make sure I wasn't accidentally going down the side passage to the air pocket like I had before.

When I came out of the cave into the open sea I looked around for Christo. I shouted his name without a lot of hope because the moonlight was bright enough for me to see that he wasn't there. I sat down on a rock and wondered what I should do next.

'Maybe Christo was only slightly injured,' I said to myself. 'Maybe he swam through the underwater passage with Karl, helping him with Sten, but something happened. Maybe he's in the air pocket!'

I stood up, filled my lungs with air, and dived back into the water. I found the side passage to the air pocket on my third attempt. I surfaced in the air pocket and took a deep breath.

'Here . . .' said a quiet voice.

'Christo! Thank God! I've been . . .'

'Richard. Help me.'

'Yes. I'm here to help.'

I pushed out my hands and touched Christo. He moaned.

'Are you badly hurt?'

'. . . I have . . . some injury.'

'You have to swim. We've got to get out of this air pocket. I'll swim ahead using my arms, and you'll have to hold on to my legs and try to kick. Understand?'

His voice sound fainter. '... I understand.'

'OK, Christo,' I said. 'I think I know which direction to take.'

Within a few strokes I realized that the passage was not the one leading back to the original cave. About ten metres along we found a second air pocket, and ten metres further on we found another. Then we came up into fresh air. I could see real stars and real sky.

I laid the exhausted Christo out on a flat rock. 'You're OK now, Christo,' I said quietly. 'You're OK.'

Chapter 7   Unwelcome Newcomers

The atmosphere in the camp had become very tense. The divisions that I'd noticed when I got back from the Rice Run seemed to be getting worse.

People had separated into different groups. There was Bugs's group – the carpenters and most of the gardeners. The first afternoon after the shark attack I found them all sitting in the centre of the clearing in a circle, smoking dope and chatting quietly. Then there were other, smaller groups. There were the people in my old fishing group and Keaty. I included myself in this group – but there was also Jed, and I included myself with him as well. Then there were the cooks. And finally there were Sal and Karl. Sal was trying extremely hard to get on with everyone, and Karl seemed to be in a world of his own after the shark incident. This, then, was the politics in the camp, and we all had to deal with the situation in our own way. If it sounds complicated, that's because it was.

◆

After work one afternoon, I walked over the hospital tent. It was actually the Swedes' tent, but Sten was dead and Karl had started living on the beach, so I'd begun calling it the hospital tent. Jed had been looking after Christo there since I'd found him in the cave.

'Back early today,' said Jed, when I went into the tent. He sounded very tired and was sweating heavily.

'I got hungry and needed a cigarette.' I looked at Christo. 'How is he?'

Jed rubbed his eyes. 'He's getting worse. He's got a bad fever and he's unconscious most of the time. When he's awake he's in a lot of pain. To tell you the truth, I'm getting seriously worried about him.'

I frowned. Christo looked OK to me. Apart from a single cut on his arm, his only wound was a large bruise on his stomach where the shark had smashed into him.

'I mean,' Jed continued, 'that bruise should be getting better, shouldn't it?'

I leant over to take a closer look at Christo's stomach.

'It's blacker than it was. Not so purple. I think that means it's healing.'

'I'm not sure . . . ,' Jed said in a worried voice.

'Well, I'm going to get some food now and find Étienne and Françoise,' I said.

'OK. Leave me a cigarette will you? And come back later. Nobody comes in to see if I'm OK apart from you. I think they're avoiding having to see Christo – pretending it hasn't happened maybe.'

I threw him a packet of cigarettes. 'Well, it's not easy for anyone. Sten's body is lying behind the longhouse and you can smell it through the walls.'

Jed looked at me sadly. 'Well, we're going to bury him tomorrow morning. By the waterfall.'

It was getting close to six o'clock when I reached the beach. I found Étienne and Keaty sitting on the sand, discussing Karl.

'He's gone completely mad,' said Keaty.

'No he hasn't,' said Étienne in an angry voice. 'He's in a state of shock. We should take him to Ko Pha-Ngan.' Then he got up and started walking away.

I'd obviously arrived in the middle of something, and I wasn't happy at all with the idea that my friends had been arguing.

'Was Étienne being serious about Ko Pha-Ngan?' I asked Keaty.

He nodded. 'He's been saying it all day. He's says he's going to discuss it with Sal.'

'But he must know we can't take Karl to Ko Pha-Ngan. What

would we say? "Here's a friend of ours who's been attacked by a shark and had a nervous breakdown on our secret beach. See you . . ."'?'

'He thinks we could just take him there and leave him on a beach.'

'That's ridiculous. Even if he didn't tell people about our beach, how would we know that he got looked after? They might just ignore him.' I shook my head. 'No, the best thing for Karl is for him to stay here.'

'I've been telling Étienne that all day. But he wants to take Sten to Ko Pha-Ngan as well,' said Keaty.

'*Sten*? But he's dead! What would be the point of . . .?'

'His family. Étienne thinks we have to let them know what's happened to their son.'

I smiled in disbelief. 'Yeah, and meanwhile we'd definitely get discovered. It's the worst idea I've ever heard.'

After all the discussion about Karl, I decided I ought to go and see him myself. Or that's what I told Keaty. Really I was just interested in finding Françoise, whom I'd hardly seen over the past few days. Following the misunderstood kiss, I hadn't wanted to give Étienne any reasons to be suspicious.

I found Françoise about four hundred metres away, sitting near Karl. When she saw me, she ran over to me, smiling.

'Richard!' she said. 'Thank you!'

I paused. '. . . What for?'

'For helping me when I was sick. You were so kind.'

'Françoise, it was nothing.'

She smiled, then looked at me straight in the eyes and laughed. 'You kissed me!'

'I thought you were sleeping . . .'

'I was. Étienne told me the next day.'

'Oh . . . well . . . I hope you don't mind . . . It was sort of complicated . . .'

63

'Of course I do not mind! But why do you say it was complicated?'

'Well . . . complicated is probably the wrong word . . . The kiss wasn't . . .' I stopped and then tried again. '. . . I'm not sure what Étienne told you, but I was kissing you because you were so ill, and then when I'd started it was hard to stop.'

'Well, I expect Étienne thought it was . . . you know . . .'

'A sexy kiss?'

'Mmm.' Françoise laughed again. Then she leant over and gave me a little kiss on the cheek. 'Was it a sexy kiss?'

'No,' I replied, lying. 'Of course not.'

'So there is no problem. Not complicated.'

'I'm glad you understand.'

'Always,' she said. 'I always understand.'

For a moment we looked at each other. Then the moment was over, broken by Françoise as she turned to look at Karl.

♦

The next day, at Sten's funeral, we all circled the grave that had been dug near the waterfall. Sal said a few words, talking about Sten's commitment to the camp and how much we'd all miss him. Then one of the cooks talked about how Sten always caught big fish which kept people's stomachs full. Someone else told us how Sten was always ready to play football on Sunday and how fairly he played.

When we began filling the grave with earth, several people started crying. Bugs planted a wooden cross on the grave with Sten's name on it.

As we all turned to go back to the camp, Sal stopped us.

'Wait,' she called out. 'I don't want anyone leaving yet. There's something important I need to say, and I want everyone to hear it.'

People stopped, looking puzzled, and waited for Sal to continue.

'OK. I'd like to start by asking everyone to sit down so you can all see me.'

We slowly sat down on the grass. Sal waited until we were all settled, then nodded. 'I want to talk about the atmosphere in the camp. I'm going to talk about it because I've got no choice. I'm going to talk about it because no one else seems willing to do so.'

No one said anything.

'The way I see things is like this,' Sal went on. 'We've had two disasters over the past week. First there was the food poisoning, and then we had the terrible tragedy with the shark. For these reasons, the atmosphere in the camp has been bad. It's understandable – we're all human. But it ends *here*! It ends with the burial of a friend, so that something positive will come out of his death.

'Now, dates don't mean much on the beach but I keep a calendar. And it may interest you to know that the date today is September the eleventh.'

As a matter of fact, it interested me a lot to hear that the date was September the eleventh, because it meant it was almost five months since I'd left England.

'That means that our special beach festival is in three days' time. As most of you know, the festival is our birthday and we celebrate it every year.'

As she said this, Sal looked rather sad. 'To be honest, I haven't been looking forward to this year's festival much. Without Daffy, I don't mind telling you that it will feel very strange. But after the trouble we've been through, particularly losing Sten, I now feel it's exactly what we need. It will remind us what we are and why we're here. As it's our birthday, it will mark a fresh start.'

Sal paused for a moment, clearly lost in thought. Then her face hardened and she continued. 'OK. So that's it. I hope you all listened hard. Tomorrow we'll start getting ready for the party.'

When we got back to the camp, I noticed that the mood had

improved. I was half expecting people to sit down in their groups and begin analysing the morning's events. But within a few minutes, everyone had left for work and the clearing was empty.

It must have been after midday before I checked on Zeph and Sammy through the binoculars. Jed had gone back to the hospital tent to look after Christo, so I was on my own again. I got to our usual rock, sat down, and put the binoculars up to my face. Quickly, I looked along the beach. Nothing! Where were they?

'Oh my God!' I shouted, when I finally saw them. There, on a raft in the sea, sailing slowly towards our island, were Zeph, Sammy and the three Germans!

I raced back to the camp, wondering who I should tell about the raft first – Jed or Sal. I decided to go and find Jed.

I noticed the bad smell as soon as I climbed into the hospital tent. It was sweet and sour.

'You get used to it,' Jed said quickly. 'In a couple of minutes you won't smell a thing. Don't go.'

I pulled up the neck of my T-shirt to cover my nose and mouth. 'I wasn't going to go.'

'Not one person has come in all day. Can you believe it? Not one person.' He turned to look at me and I frowned with concern when I saw his face. Although his suntan was still deep, his face looked grey as if his blood had lost its colour. 'I've been listening to them out there since two o'clock. They've been playing football! None of them have been thinking about Christo!'

I nodded, although actually I was only half listening. He clearly needed to talk, but I had to tell him about the raft. Sammy and Zeph would arrive on our island before nightfall. At the earliest, that meant they could start the journey across the island tomorrow morning, and could reach the beach by tomorrow afternoon.

Christo moved and for a second his eyes opened. Jed wiped his forehead gently.

'How long will he be like this?' I asked.

'Two days . . .'

'Well that's good. If Christo's better in two days he can talk to Karl and . . .'

Jed shook his head. 'No,' he said quietly. 'You don't understand. Christo's not getting better. In two days he'll be dead.'

'He's dying? But . . . how do you know?'

Jed pulled back the sheet that covered Christo's body. 'Feel there,' he said, pointing to Christo's stomach.

The entire area of his stomach was almost completely black and as hard as a rock.

'He's been bleeding inside,' said Jed. 'Bleeding badly. I couldn't be sure until last night.'

'Who else knows?'

'Just you and Sal . . . and Bugs too, probably. I talked to Sal today. She said that now we've started to get things back to normal, nobody must find out.'

Jed stroked Christo's shoulder before pulling back the sheet. We sat in silence for a minute or two, watching his shallow breathing. It was strange that, after Jed had explained, it was obvious to me that he was dying. The smell I'd noticed as I'd entered the tent was the smell of death.

I suddenly remembered the raft and broke the silence.

'Zeph and Sammy have built a raft. They're on their way!'

Jed didn't move. 'If they get to the beach,' he said, 'they'll see Christo die. Everything here will be destroyed.' And that was all.

I left the tent and walked close to the longhouse entrance, past where Sal sat talking with Bugs, and continued along to the beach path. At the first corner I stopped, leaning against a tree, and lit a cigarette. Sal appeared almost at once.

'Something's happened,' she said. 'What is it?'

Before I could reply she said, 'They're on their way, aren't they?'

'Yes.'

'Oh my God! When do you think they'll get here?'

'Sometime tomorrow afternoon, if they don't get frightened by the dope guards,' I answered. 'They built a raft.'

'Have you told anyone about this?'

'Only Jed.'

'OK, Richard. It looks like we have a slight problem here. But you don't think they can possibly get here until tomorrow, do you?'

'No.'

'Then I'm going to think about this overnight. I'll give you my decision on what we do about them in the morning.'

I put my head into the hospital tent before going to bed in the longhouse. Jed was fast asleep, but Christo was half awake. He even recognized me.

'Richard,' he whispered.

'Yes,' I whispered back. 'How are you feeling?'

'I feel very bad, Richard. Very bad.'

'I know. But you'll be better soon.'

'Sten . . .'

'You'll see him in the morning.'

'My chest . . .'

'Close your eyes.'

'Very bad . . .'

'Shh now.'

He nodded and at last his eyes shut.

'Have good dreams,' I said, maybe too quietly for him to hear.

I left the tent door open when I left. I wanted to stop Jed breathing too much of that dying air.

Chapter 8   Paradise to Hell

Sal gave me my instructions at a quarter to six the next morning. I had to follow Zeph, Sammy and the three other rafters across the island. When they reached the top of the waterfall, she wanted me to stop them and tell them to leave the island at once. If that didn't work, I had to prevent them from going any further, in any way I could, until Christo was dead. After that, we would work out whether to let them into the camp or keep them out.

By setting off early, I was hoping that Zeph and Sammy would still be with their raft. Finding them would be a lot harder if they'd already entered the jungle. I was also assuming that they'd have landed on the same stretch of beach where Étienne, Françoise and I had first arrived.

The early-morning effort was worth it. The rafters were still on the beach. Even though I'd been watching them for weeks, it was a shock to see the group so near. It confirmed that it actually was Zeph and Sammy we'd been watching, and therefore that I was responsible for their presence on the island. I still hadn't worked out what I was going to say to Sal about the map.

From where I was lying – about twenty metres from where they sat – I could see only four of them. The fifth was hidden behind the raft. One of the Germans I could see was a boy, the other a girl. With some satisfaction, I saw that the girl was pretty but not as pretty as Françoise. No one on the beach was as pretty as Françoise. The guy looked very similar to Bugs – they could have been brothers. I disliked him immediately.

Eventually I managed to see the fifth person in the group. Another girl, and annoyingly I couldn't criticize her looks. She had a lovely figure, very long brown hair, and an attractive quiet laugh that travelled across the sand to where I lay.

The rafters didn't make the same mistake as I had with Étienne and Françoise – walking along the coast before realizing that the only way to get to the other side of the island was to go inland. But later, they made a far more serious mistake.

Actually, I knew they were going to make the mistake even before it happened. Firstly, they hadn't hidden their raft properly. And secondly, they chatted loudly as they walked. To me this clearly suggested one thing: they were entirely unaware of any need for caution.

When they arrived at the dope field, not one of them realized they were in a field. Sammy shouted out, 'Man! I've never seen so much dope! There's more dope here than I've ever seen!' He started tearing big handfuls of leaves off the plants and throwing them in the air. Then the other four started shouting and throwing leaves in the air too. They looked like million-dollar bank robbers throwing money around. Completely out of control. It was ten o'clock. The guards would have been on duty for two hours at least, and if they hadn't heard the rafters crashing though the jungle, they'd certainly hear them now.

By chance, I was hiding in the same bush that I'd hidden in with Étienne and Françoise. Watching Zeph and Sammy was like watching myself – what could have happened six months ago if Étienne hadn't acted so sensibly. It looked like the problem with our uninvited guests was going to be solved, and I was also going to find out what happened when the dope guards caught someone. Better than that, I was actually going to see it.

I wouldn't want anyone to think that I was without pity for them. I didn't want Zeph and Sammy on the island and I knew it would be convenient if they disappeared, but it didn't have to be this way. The ideal would be: they arrived, I had a couple of days following them as they found their way across the island, then they gave up at the waterfall and went back home. I would have had some fun, and there'd have been no spilt tears and no spilt blood.

Zeph bled like a pig. When the guards appeared, he'd begun walking straight over towards them like they were old friends. To me it was a crazy thing to do, but that's what he did. He *still* hadn't realized what was going on, even though all the guards were pointing their guns at him. Maybe he thought they were part of our community, or maybe he was so shocked that he just didn't realize how much trouble he was in. But it didn't matter what he thought. As soon as he got close, one of the guards smashed him hard in the face. I wasn't surprised. The guard looked very nervous and just as confused by Zeph's strange behaviour as I was.

After that there were a few seconds of silence while the guards and the rafters stared at each other across the top of the dope plants. It seemed as if each of the two groups was as shocked as the other. The rafters were having to make a huge mental adjustment. Paradise to Hell in a few seconds. The dope guards seemed amazed that anyone could be stupid enough to walk into their field and start tearing leaves off their plants.

It occurred to me that most of the guards were more like country boys than experienced fighters. I think in some ways it made them seem more dangerous. Maybe someone more experienced wouldn't have panicked and smashed Zeph's face in. Don't people say that the only thing more dangerous than a man with a gun is a nervous man with a gun? It was certainly true in this case. When the short period of staring was over, the guards began violently beating the rafters. I suppose they might have beaten them to death right there, but another group of guards suddenly arrived, and this group appeared to have a boss. I'd never seen him before. He was older than the others. One word from him, and the beating stopped.

'Who are you?' he said, in English, very loudly and clearly.

A difficult question. What do you say? Do you formally introduce yourself, do you say 'no one', do you beg for your life?

I thought Sammy handled it very well, considering that, like Zeph, he'd just had his front teeth knocked out.

'We're travellers from Ko Pha-Ngan,' he replied. 'We were looking for some other travellers. We made a mistake. We didn't know this was your island.'

The boss nodded, not unkindly. 'Very big mistake.'

'Please, we're very sorry.'

'You alone now? And friends here now?'

'We're alone. We were looking for a friend. We thought he was here, and we know we made a mist–'

'Why you look for friend here?'

'Our friend gave us a map.'

'What map?'

'I can show–'

'You can show me map. Later.'

'Please. We're very sorry.'

'Yes. I know about you being sorry.'

'We'd like to go. We could leave your island now and we wouldn't tell anyone about anything.'

'Yes. You tell no one. I know about that.'

Sammy tried to smile. All his remaining teeth were bright red. 'Will you let us go? Please.'

'Ah.' The boss smiled back. 'You can go.'

'Thank you, sir, thank you. I promise you, we won't tell any–'

'You can go with us.'

'With you?'

'You go with us now.'

'No,' Sammy began to protest. 'Please, wait, we made a mistake! We're *very* sorry! We won't tell *anyone*!'

The German guy started to get up, holding his arms in the air. 'We will not speak!' he cried. 'We will not speak!'

The boss stared at the German, then spoke quickly to the guards. Three of them moved forward and tried to lift Zeph by

72

the arms. He began to struggle. Another guard stepped forward and hit him in the stomach. The other rafters began screaming. One of the German girls tried to run away, but the guards caught her and started beating her.

I covered my face in my hands as the guards began dragging their prisoners away.

The cries and screams were gradually replaced by jungle noises. I slowly stood up and set off on my way back to the camp. It wasn't an easy journey. My head ached, my legs felt unsteady, and I kept falling over.

Looking back, it seems obvious that I'd suffered a terrible trauma and was in a hurry to leave an area which still felt heavy with screams. But that wasn't how I saw it at the time. I only thought about the importance of getting back to the camp and telling Sal about what had happened.

After a few minutes I heard a loud noise from somewhere in the jungle. I froze. Within five or six seconds the silence was exploded by a burst of gunfire. The noise tore through the trees with shocking loudness.

'Jesus Christ . . .' I whispered to myself. 'It's happened. They've been shot.' I felt violently sick. I imagined the rafters' bodies, their shirts covered in blood, their limbs twisted.

As I made my way down to the waterfall, I couldn't decide if it had all gone wrong or if it had all gone right. It was true that our problem with the new arrivals was over, and that Sal would never find out that I'd given Zeph and Sammy the map. But that didn't seem to change the way I was feeling. Struggling to walk, I wanted to scream out loud. My brain couldn't cope with what had just happened – it refused to even try.

Sal was waiting for me beneath the waterfall. 'What the hell happened?' she said, more angry than anxious. 'Why did I hear gunshots?'

'The rafters,' I said.

'They've been killed?'

'Yes. I saw them get caught by the guards and then later I heard the firing.'

'You didn't see it?'

'No.'

'What happened when they were caught?'

'They were beaten. Badly.'

'Badly enough to scare them? Maybe just a message?'

'Worse.'

'Then?'

'They got taken away somewhere. Dragged.'

'Dragged . . . You didn't follow?'

'No.'

'What next?'

'The shooting . . .'

'I see . . .' Sal stared at me. 'Badly beaten, you say . . .'

'Very badly.'

'You feel responsible for their deaths?'

I thought about this before replying, not wanting Sal to discover my connection to Zeph and Sammy at this late stage. 'It was their decision to come here,' I said eventually. 'They made a lot of noise in the jungle. It was their fault.'

Sal nodded. 'Others may have heard the shooting. What will you tell them?'

'Nothing.'

'I think Étienne might know that Christo's dying. He's being difficult again . . .'

'I won't tell Étienne,' I interrupted. 'I won't tell Françoise or Keaty or anyone . . . Except Jed . . . You know I'll tell Jed.'

'Of course I do Richard,' Sal said. 'But it's nice of you to ask permission.' Then she suddenly turned and walked away. She didn't even wait for me, or hear me whisper, 'Actually, I wasn't asking for your permission.'

I didn't follow Sal back to the camp because I didn't want to see anyone yet. In fact, I didn't want to do anything much. Except maybe sleep. I wanted to get away from my brain that was still making me want to scream. The trouble was, if I slept I'd dream, and I knew I'd have terrible dreams.

In the end I talked to myself. Walking near the waterfall, I asked my mind to leave me alone for a while. I was trying to find some peace and quiet, but it didn't work. So I tried to get interested in a pretty flower or the patterns on a tree. But that failed too.

No place to avoid thinking. I realized this eventually and started to walk straight into the jungle so that I could reach the beach without crossing the clearing.

I'll keep this short. Absolutely limited to what I can remember. My memory of the next few minutes isn't very good. No doubt a result of the morning's trauma and my state of mind.

'The rafters are dead,' I said to Karl, when I'd found him on the beach. 'Christo will be dead within forty-eight hours. All our problems are over except one. It's time you got sane.'

Karl looked at me, or he looked through me, or he wasn't looking at anything at all. I didn't really care. I took a step towards him, and as I did so he hit out viciously at my legs. The blow hurt, so I hit him back.

I sat on his chest, my knees against his upper arms, trying to push a handful of rice into his mouth. He made sounds, probably words. 'That's right!' I shouted. 'I'm making you better now!' His fingers went round my neck. I pushed them away. I think I may have lost the rice in the struggle. I think I may have been holding sand.

I assume I closed my eyes. Instead of Karl's face, I have a mental picture of a red-brown blanket. Nothingness, so I think I must have closed my eyes. Then a blue blanket, then a red-brown blanket again.

I sat up. Karl was twenty or more metres down the beach, running like crazy. Amazed that he could still have so much strength after days of starvation, I leapt to my feet and raced after him.

Down the beach, through the trees, up the path, into the clearing, I'd nearly caught him. I was just going to get hold of his hair when I tripped over something and he escaped.

I got up quickly. Several people were standing nearby, watching. 'Catch him!' I shouted. But they were too shocked to react. 'You fools! He's getting away!' A few seconds later, he'd disappeared.

I fell down on my knees and started banging the ground with my fists.

A light hand touched my shoulder. I looked round and saw Françoise leaning over me, and behind her a group of curious people. 'Richard?' she said anxiously. 'Are you OK?'

'Yes,' I began, and then stopped, trying to remember what had happened. 'I think Karl ... attacked me.'

'You are hurt?' said Françoise.

'I'm fine.'

'Why did he do it?'

'I ... I really don't know ...' I shook my head in desperation. I didn't feel at all ready to cope with these questions. 'Maybe ... maybe he thought I was a fish. He was a fisher and ... he's mad ...'

Then everyone started talking at once.

'I should have caught him,' someone said. 'He ran so close!'

'I saw the look in his eye! He looked right at me! It was awful!'

'We should catch him and tie him up!'

Only one voice disagreed: Étienne's. 'This is impossible,' he shouted above the others. 'I do not believe Karl would attack Richard! I do not believe it! I was with him this morning!'

The others stopped talking and listened.

'This morning I was with him for one hour! One hour, and

he ate rice with me! He was getting better! I know he would not attack anyone!'

I frowned in disbelief. 'Are you saying I'm a liar?'

Étienne hesitated, then turned away from me, talking to the others. 'For one hour I was with him! He said my name! For the first time in a week he talked! I *know* he was getting better!'

Suddenly I began to agree with Étienne, just wanting to get away.

'Yes. Étienne's right. It may have been my fault. I could have frightened him –'

Sal interrupted sharply. 'No! I'm afraid Karl has become dangerous. This morning I also went to see him, and he tried to hit me too.'

Surprised, I studied her expression hard. Was she lying or telling the truth?

'Luckily Bugs was there to stop him. I should have warned you but I was trying to work out the best way to deal with him. I didn't want to spoil our birthday celebration with more bad news. I was stupid, but things had been going so well . . .'

'Well we can't have someone as dangerous as that just wandering around,' someone said. 'Something will have to be done.'

Everyone nodded, and for some strange reason, I felt they were all nodding at me.

'I know,' said Sal. 'You're quite right.'

'No!' cried Étienne desperately, his arms out in front of him as if he was begging us to listen. 'Please! Please, everybody *must* listen! Karl is not dangerous! He needs help! I think maybe we could take him to Ko Pha . . .'

This time it was Françoise who made him stop, by walking away. He couldn't speak as he watched her marching across the clearing. Then he ran after her, still holding his arms out in front of him.

When it was dark, I went over to the hospital tent. If possible, conditions were even worse inside the tent than they had been before. The terrible smell was the same, but now there was blood everywhere. Blood from Christo's stomach on the sheets, all over the floor, and across Jed's arms and chest.

'Jesus Christ,' I said. 'What's been going on in here?'

Jed turned towards me. He looked terrible. 'Do you have any good news?' he asked in a low voice. 'I'm tired of bad news now. I only want to hear good news.'

I paused. 'I've got some news. Zeph and Sammy are dead. Shot by the dope guards.'

'Dead,' Jed said, without emotion.

'Aren't you pleased? Not pleased, I mean relieved . . . in a way. It means the beach is safe. Our secret beach.'

'What about the others?' he asked.

'The others?'

'The people we haven't seen yet. The ones that will arrive next week, next month, or next year, and the ones that will arrive after them,' he said in a tired voice.

Chapter 9   Escape!

I watched Sal from just inside the longhouse door. Everyone was standing in a big circle and she was in the middle, marching around and shouting out orders. The fishers had to catch extra fish for the party meal; Bugs and the carpenters had to build an eating area; the cooks had to cook seven whole chickens.

Watching Sal's skilful organization, I wondered how she'd react if I explained to her what Jed had said. That, despite all our efforts to protect the beach, other people like Zeph and Sammy would come in the future. I wondered if the thought would frighten her as much as it frightened me.

When everyone had woken that morning in the longhouse, I'd pretended to be asleep. It didn't take long for them all to leave, and I was able to sit up and have a cigarette.

By eight, the camp had been given their duties for the day's preparations and everyone was busy working around the clearing. It was past eight-thirty when Sal appeared in the entrance to the longhouse.

'You're being missed,' she said, walking up to me. 'Françoise has asked me to make certain you join them as soon as you wake up.'

'What about Jed?' I asked quickly.

'I haven't seen him yet. But I'm sure he'd like to see you too.' I noticed a slightly worried expression on her face. 'There was something else I was hoping you might do, Richard. You see, I know it may feel as if, with our rafters gone, our troubles are over. But I'm afraid they aren't. We still have the problem of the Swedes.' She paused and touched her hair. 'Now, if Christo dies during the festival, no one has to know. I think our real problem is—'

'Karl.'

'Karl. That's right. And I'm afraid you'll have to take responsibility for him.'

'Me?'

'Yes, you're quite right to look guilty.'

'Guilty?'

'If you hadn't disturbed him, he'd have stayed on the beach all through today and tonight, and through next week as well I expect. Of course, we'd have had to deal with him at some point, but I was planning to leave the matter until after the festival. Because of what you did, we have to act now.' She gestured in the direction of the clearing. 'Take a look out there. You can see how important the celebrations are to everyone here. We must make sure they go well . . .'

With a shock, I realized what she was going to ask me to do.

'Let me explain the problem, Richard. Karl's wandering around like a madman, and he might suddenly appear and—'

'Sal,' I interrupted. 'I won't do it.'

There was a short silence. I could sense that Sal was thinking fast. Eventually she crossed her arms. 'You won't do what, Richard?'

'I won't, Sal. I won't do it.'

'Do what?'

'Don't ask me, please . . .'

I looked at her carefully, wondering if I'd misunderstood her. But as my eyes moved to her face, she looked away, and I knew for certain I was right. She wanted me to find Karl and kill him!

'I'm afraid I *am* asking you, Richard.'

I shook my head. 'Sal, please . . .'

'I'm going to leave the longhouse now. In half an hour I'll come back and you will be gone. By tonight, all of our troubles will be behind us. The last month will be finished. We'll never have to think about it ever again.' She stood up. 'The beach is my life, Richard, but it's yours too. Don't forget that.'

I nodded miserably.

'Good.' She returned the nod, turned around, and walked away.

Outside the longhouse, everyone was busy in the clearing. Most people were helping to prepare vegetables. The carpenters were in the middle, getting the eating area ready. All working and laughing. I easily managed to walk out of the jungle-side of the longhouse without being seen.

I thought of the caves after I'd looked for Karl around the waterfall. If I'd been thinking more clearly I would have checked the caves first. But it wouldn't have made much difference. The boat had probably been gone for hours.

These days I can find comfort in the idea that my attack on Karl on the beach had cured him. I often picture him, trying to guess what he's doing at this moment or that. I imagine him having a normal life in Sweden – skiing, eating, working in an office, drinking with friends in a bar.

But at the time my reaction wasn't so simple. Part of me was relieved that I couldn't now kill Karl. Most of me, however, was in shock. For the first few minutes, after realizing that Karl had taken the boat and escaped from our island, I couldn't even climb out of the water on to the rocks. I couldn't imagine how Sal would react to this development. What would happen when Karl arrived on Ko Pha-Ngan?

Eventually I managed to pull myself out of the water and sat on a rock. I didn't move again until, a short while later, I saw someone surface near the underwater passage.

'Richard?' the head called over the sound of the waves. It was Étienne. 'Are you here, Richard?'

I stood up and waved to him. He swam over and joined me on the rock. After at least half a minute, he began to speak.

'Richard, I want to talk to you, but . . . I do not know . . .'

'You don't know what?' I asked.

He took a deep breath. 'I do not know if it is . . . safe.'

'*Safe*?'

'I think you . . . do things. You do things for Sal. Today you were looking for Karl . . .'

I felt sick and closed my eyes.

'Is he dead now?' Étienne asked.

Étienne might have continued speaking, asking what I'd done with Karl, but I can't be sure because I wasn't really listening. I was thinking about the food poisoning, Sten's forgotten funeral, Christo dying in the death tent, Karl wandering around the beach, and the terrible shooting of the rafters. My mind was filling up with all these traumas and I was hit by a wave of sickness.

'Étienne,' I said, hearing my voice from far away. 'Would you like to go home?'

He didn't seem to reply for a long time. 'You mean . . . the camp?'

'Not the camp. I mean home. Leaving the beach. France for you and Françoise, England for me.'

I turned to face him and saw the expression of hope and fear on his face.

'Don't worry,' I said. 'Everything will be OK. We're going to leave tonight.'

I wasn't worried about the practicalities of leaving. It would have been easier if Karl hadn't taken the boat, but we still had the raft. If that was gone, we'd swim. We were all much fitter than we had been and I was sure we could manage the swim to the next island again. We had water and we knew how to catch fish to eat. I had much more serious things on my mind – like who we'd take with us.

Françoise was the first person we had to talk to. We found her on the beach. Étienne stood in front of her, talking rapidly in French. After a few minutes Françoise looked over at me with wide eyes. Étienne said something urgent, and she answered. Then he nodded quickly in my direction, and that was that. I knew she'd agreed to leave the island with us.

It was a big relief. I'd been completely unable to predict how she'd react, and so had Étienne. But the other two names on our list were even more unpredictable – Jed and Keaty. Or my list, I should say, because Étienne didn't want to take either of them. I could understand that – if we had only had Françoise to take, we could almost have left at once. But over the months of my beach life, Jed and Keaty had been my two best friends, and I couldn't disappear without offering them the chance to come too.

Soon after Étienne had finished talking to Françoise, she came over to where I sat.

'Is there a problem?' I asked.

'No,' she said. 'But, Richard, you do not think things can get better after the festival? Everyone says life will be better. You do not think, maybe we should stay? We can wait for a few more days, and then . . .'

'The festival will change nothing, Françoise. Life will only get worse.'

'Worse . . . worse than we have had?'

'Yes.'

'But you will not tell me why.'

'I don't think I can explain but I'm sure I'm right.'

'We will never be able to come back,' she said. 'So sad . . .'

'Perhaps,' I replied, 'if there was anything to come back to.'

She walked away and I went to find Keaty. I'd imagined that he would be the hardest to persuade. He'd lived on the beach for longer than all of us. But in fact he was the easiest. All I had to do was tell him that the boat had disappeared.

'Oh my God! What's Sal going to say? She'll go mad! Jesus Christ!'

'What's wrong?' I asked.

'I was the one who tied the boat up,' he said. He'd been to Ko Pha-Ngan in the boat with Bugs to buy things for the celebration meal. 'First the dead squid, now losing the boat! She'll kill me!'

'Keaty . . .'

'Does Sal know about the boat already?'

'No.'

'You promise?'

'I promise. But she'll find out soon.'

'And then what will she do? I'll have to . . .'

'Leave?'

'I'll have to leave! Yes! Jesus! I should leave right now! I'll take the boat . . . Oh, God, I can't. I'm trapped here . . . trapped . . .'

'No,' I replied. 'There might be another way.'

I was beginning to feel in control. Now I only had to find Jed, tell him about the plan, and wait for our chance to escape. I was feeling so good that I started singing as Keaty and I walked into the clearing. Then Keaty started singing too.

'What are you doing?' I whispered as I suddenly realized that people were looking at us. 'Shut up! We've got to act normally. We don't want anyone to find out about our plan. If Sal asks you to help with the preparations for the meal, just try to be calm.'

'OK,' Keaty whispered, and walked off to his tent, swinging his arms by his sides.

Étienne and Françoise were coping better, but they did have each other for support. They sat close to the kitchen hut, chatting and helping prepare the enormous catch of fish.

Sal came up to me almost as soon as I entered the clearing.

'I'm glad to see you're happier than this morning,' she said.

'I feel much better.'

'Good . . . I assume that means that I shouldn't worry about any unexpected problems tonight at the party.'

'That's right,' I answered. 'No problems. You can ... forget about him.'

'Forget?' Sal said. 'Forget about who?'

'Karl.'

She gave me an odd look. 'Who?'

'Karl.'

'Who's Karl?'

'Karl's ...' I began, then I realized what she meant. 'Nobody.'

'I thought you were talking about someone here.'

'No.'

'Fine.' Sal nodded. 'Well, I'd better get back to work. Still lots to do.'

A few moments later she was standing in the middle of the clearing, talking to Bugs.

It was after four o'clock before I had a chance to get to the hospital tent to talk to Jed, and a chance to do something else as well.

At four, all the preparations for the evening were finished and Sal suggested a game of football down on the beach. This was excellent news. Keaty and I never joined in the football, so no one thought it was odd when we remained behind in the camp. We offered to stir the food in the cooking pots while the others were gone.

By ten past four the clearing was empty and I was putting large handfuls of dope into the pots.

'The cooks will notice,' said Keaty nervously. 'It's going to taste really strange.'

'If they notice, I'll just admit it was me. I'll say it was for the atmosphere,' I said. 'If we don't do this, the party will go on all night and we'll never be able to escape. This way, after about an hour everyone will be too stoned to notice what we're doing. Just make sure you don't eat any of this. Only eat the chicken and rice. And make sure Étienne and Françoise do the same.'

When I walked into the hospital tent, the atmosphere was like in a church. The sort of atmosphere where you feel uncomfortable if you cough or move too quickly.

Amazingly, Christo was still breathing. Jed's hair and beard were completely covered in blood and sweat. He didn't look at me when I came into the tent. His eyes were fixed on Christo's calm face.

'Jed,' I said gently. 'There's something we should talk about.'

'You're leaving,' he said.

'Yes!'

'When?'

'Tonight. When everyone's asleep or stoned. Will you come?'

'If Christo's dead.'

'And if he isn't?'

'I'll stay.'

'You understand that unless you come tonight, there'll be no way off the island.'

'Mmm.'

'And the problem isn't going to be more travellers coming here. Karl's taken the boat. If he contacts his family or Sten and Christo's families . . .'

'The police will come.'

'Yes. And you won't be able to escape.'

'I know.'

'I want you to come. It makes no difference to Christo if you're here or not. You know that too, don't you? Most of his brain has already shut down.'

'He isn't dead until he stops breathing.'

'OK . . .' I thought hard for a couple of seconds. 'So why don't we stop him breathing? We could cover up his mouth. It would only take five minutes.'

'No.'

'You don't have to do it. I'll do it for you. You could hold his

86

hand or something. It would be a nice way for him to die. Very peaceful and –'

'Listen, Richard,' said Jed, looking at me for the first time. 'Christo should be dead by tonight, so I should be able to come with you. Why don't you go back to the others now? I don't think Sal would like it if you were in here.'

'But –'

'Come and check before you leave,' he said, and turned back to Christo. I stayed for a minute, and then left the tent.

The rest of the camp had begun returning to the clearing. Singing, laughing, arm in arm. The party was going to start.

There were four circles in the middle of the clearing. First a ring of candles, then our plates, then all of us, then another circle of candles. It looked marvellous and very, very frightening. Orange faces in the candlelight and clouds of dope smoke. And a lot of noise. People weren't talking, they were shouting. Sometimes screaming. Just telling jokes, asking for more food – but it sounded like screaming.

They were all drinking heavily. The cooks had made a drink from coconut milk. You make it like this: Take a green coconut, still up in the tree, and make a small cut in its base. Under the cut, hang a bowl to catch the milk. Then leave it for a few hours. When you come back, you'll find that the milk has fermented, and that if you drink it you'll get very drunk. A clever trick. It tastes OK – a bit sugary, but OK. I was surprised I'd never seen it done before.

I'd made us all sit together. That way I could make sure the others only ate the chicken and rice and didn't get stoned or drunk.

After half an hour, at about quarter to nine, I went to see what was happening in the hospital tent. To my amazement, Jed was asleep.

'Jed,' I said, but he didn't move. I said it louder, again with no

87

response. I knew this was my chance. I quickly moved over to Christo's head, pinched his nose and covered his mouth. A few minutes later I took my hands away, counted to 120, and crept back to the cool outdoors. And that was it. It really was as simple as that.

As I returned to the clearing, I saw that several people had started dancing. It was a nice moment. Watching the couples reminded me of the way things used to be on the beach. Sal was dancing with Bugs. She looked like a completely different person.

'You do not recognize her,' Gregorio said to me. While I'd been killing Christo, he'd sat down in my place so that he could chat to Keaty.

'No.'

'That's because tonight is our birthday, and Sal will only get stoned once a year at this party. The rest of the year, her mind is always clear. We get stoned but she keeps her mind clear for us.'

'She cares about the beach very much.'

'Very much,' Greg said. 'Of course.' He smiled and stood up. 'I will get us some more food. You would like some?'

Both Keaty and I said no.

'Just for me then,' he said, and wandered off towards the cooking pots.

Ten o'clock. The dancing had stopped. Everyone was acting very strangely – stoned from the dope I'd put in the food and the joints they'd all been smoking.

'It's weird watching them when you're not stoned,' Keaty whispered to me. 'They all look crazy.'

'It can't just be the dope,' I said. 'Even eating it, dope wouldn't make them as stoned as *that*. It must be the coconut drink.'

'Yes,' said Étienne. 'Really, I do not like this. When can we go?'

I checked my watch for the hundredth time. I'd thought we could leave at about two or three in the morning, when there'd be a bit of light creeping into the sky. But Étienne was right. I didn't like the way things were going either, and we could probably set off while it was still dark.

'In an hour,' I said. 'I think we might be able to leave in an hour.'

But at ten-thirty, things started to go wrong.

Bugs, who'd been sitting dreamily with Sal, drinking and smoking, suddenly jumped to his feet. His eyes were wide and there was an expression of terror on his face.

Everyone turned to look at him.

'What was that *noise*?'

Gregorio laughed. 'Can you hear noises, Bug?'

'It was . . . a branch being pushed. It was somebody pushing through branches.'

Sal sat up on her knees. 'Are we all here?' she said, looking round.

'Somebody is definitely out there,' Bugs said.

'Maybe it's Karl . . .' someone suggested.

Several heads turned to me.

'It isn't Karl,' I assured them.

'Jed?'

'Jed's in the hospital tent.'

'Well, if it isn't Karl or Jed . . .'

'Wait!' someone shouted. 'I heard something! . . . There!'

We all listened.

'It's nothing,' Sal began to say. 'Will you all relax? It's just the dope and coconut . . .'

'It's not,' Bugs interrupted. 'Everyone, stand up. I'm telling you – people are coming.'

'*People*?'

And suddenly we were all rising to our feet, because we could all hear the noise. It was unmistakable. People, pushing through branches, walking on leaves, coming our way from the waterfall path!

'Run!' Sal shouted. 'Everyone run! Now!'

Too late.

A figure came out of the trees within four metres of us. In seconds, more dope guards appeared by his side. They all had guns, pointing straight at us.

I turned to look around me. Everyone in the camp was staring at the guns, frozen in fright. I realized that escape was not an option now and that we were all going to get killed. As I turned back to the dope guards, I saw the boss point a finger at me. The next moment, one of his men dragged me out of the circle and forced me to the ground. Shocked, I realized I was going to get shot first!

First! If I had to get shot, then tenth, eleventh, twelfth – fine. But *first*. I couldn't believe it.

'Ah.' The boss nodded. 'You the boy always come to see us . . . Every day, ha? You like to come see us.'

I stared at him in terror. Then, to my surprise, he knelt beside me and touched my hair gently.

'Funny boy in trees, every day. We like you too. Take some dope, ha? Some dope for your friends.'

'Hurry up and kill me,' I said bravely.

'Kill you? Ah, funny boy . . . I no kill you now.' He got up. 'I no kill anyone now. I give you warning. You people here, that OK for me. One year, two year, three year, no problem ha?'

If he was waiting for a reply, none came. This seemed to make him angry. He reached into his pocket and pulled out a piece of paper. '*You making maps!*' he screamed. '*Maps bring new people! New people here! New people are danger for me! That is bad danger for you!*'

Then he dropped the map on the ground and fired a shot into it. The shot missed but it was close enough to send the paper flying into the air. 'So, my friends. You listen to my warning. Next time I will kill you all.'

He looked down at me on the ground, and then kicked me.

Hard. I tried to stand up but he hit me again. For a few seconds I was conscious, staring at his shoes. Then everything went black.

◆

I didn't know what was going on. Why wasn't anyone helping me? If I'd been unconscious, as I guessed I had, then they'd had plenty of time to come over and help me. But no one had.

I finally managed to get on to my feet – and then I saw why no one had moved.

The dope guards had left us with a reminder, just in case we hadn't listened to their warning. The bodies of the dead rafters. Bullets had done terrible things to them. All the bodies were covered in massive holes. Death had made them go stiff, and they were in strange positions.

I don't see any need to describe them in detail. I've only described them as much as I have because it's relevant to what happened next.

To have been faced with such a sight would have been bad at the best of times. Directly following the scene with the dope guards made it worse. But to go through all that while you were stoned and drunk – it would drive anyone crazy.

'Right,' Sal said eventually, and began to walk towards the pile of bodies. 'I think we should get this cleaned up. It won't take long if we all . . .'

The German guy was trapped beneath Zeph's chest, and his arms were hooking the two of them together. Sal couldn't make him move. We all watched in silence as she pulled uselessly at the German's legs.

'What a mess,' Sal said, and gave another hard pull.

She fell backwards, twisting as she fell, and landed on Sammy's body.

'Clumsy,' she exclaimed brightly.

Then she started screaming. It was a terrible sound. Bugs

91

called her name and started crying. He ran over to the eating area and grabbed one of the cook's knives. Then he went over to Sammy and started to attack him.

It began with kicking, which quickly became stabbing. In the chest, the arms, anywhere. Then he stood on Sammy's body and began pulling at his neck. Or that's what I thought he was doing. It wasn't completely clear through the shadows and most of the view was blocked by Bug's back. I only saw what he'd done when he stood up. He'd cut Sammy's head off. He'd cut if off, and was swinging it by the hair.

And suddenly someone else had a knife and was cutting the thin German girl's stomach open. Then someone else joined them and started work on Zeph. Within seconds the bodies were covered with people attacking them.

Looking back, I know that we could have left at that moment. No one would have tried to stop us. But we didn't move. We just stood and stared in horror as the rafters' bodies were viciously attacked.

I don't know how long it lasted. It could have been as long as half an hour. But at some point, I noticed that people had stopped and were sitting on the ground, exhausted.

I was watching Bugs when I heard Sal's voice. 'Wait on Chaweng for three days,' she read in a cold voice. 'If we haven't come back by then it means we made it to the beach. See you there? Richard.'

It took some time for me to understand. Several seconds passed in which the words meant nothing to me. Then I realized that she was standing beside me, holding the map I'd drawn for Zeph and Sammy.

'Richard?' someone whispered. 'Richard brought the people here?'

People came up, quietly surrounding me. Desperately, I began to search for a friendly face.

'Étienne! Françoise!' I shouted.

The others laughed.

'Sal, *please*,' I said, as I felt the first knife go into my leg. I'd been stabbed. I cried out and was stabbed again. A centimetre into the skin, this time my arm. I screamed and cried out, and then lost consciousness again.

◆

I looked around and saw Jed standing beside me. And beside him, Keaty, Étienne and Françoise. The four of them carried fishing spears.

'*You all keep back!*' Jed shouted. He reached down, lifted my arm over his shoulders, and dragged me up. '*Keep back.*'

And amazingly, they all did. They could easily have prevented us leaving if they'd wanted to, but they let us go. I don't think it was because of Sal, who had closed her eyes and couldn't seem to breathe. It was because they were tired. Their empty eyes told me that. Tired of everything.

Chapter 10 Strange but True

I feel I should provide an account of how we all got back home. But it's going to be brief because the story's finished.

We talked a lot. That's what I remember most, the talking. The first part of the journey – the night-time journey to the raft – was silent. But it was only because we were afraid of being heard by the guards. As soon as we'd left the island and were on our way, we opened our mouths and never shut them. The funny thing is, I can't really remember what we talked about. Maybe because we talked about everything, maybe because we talked about nothing.

Because of my condition, I wasn't much help, but the others managed the raft in pairs. A few hours after dawn broke, a fishing boat came to check who we were. After a bit of chat, they took us back to Ko Samui. It was extraordinary. They didn't seem curious about what we were doing on a raft in the Gulf of Thailand. We were just another group of weird travellers to them.

On Ko Samui we needed money, so Keaty and I sold our watches. Then Étienne stole a wallet. The cash was enough to get us all back to Bangkok, talking all the way.

In Bangkok, the only thing left to do was to phone home. We took turns in a phone box on the Khao San Road. We were all crying by the time we'd finished.

Seventy-two hours later, we had air tickets and replacement passports from our embassies. The cuts on my body still felt bad as I was buying cigarettes at the airport. As soon as we boarded the plane, I felt OK.

♦

At this exact moment, I'm sitting in front of a computer. At this exact moment, I'm typing this sentence. At this exact moment, it's a year and a month since I flew out of Thailand.

I never saw Étienne and Françoise again. One day I will. It's going to be by chance, but I know it's going to happen because the world is a small place and Europe is even smaller.

I see Keaty and Jed all the time, and they see each other even more. This is strange but true: they both work at the same place. Different companies, same building.

What else?

About three months ago, maybe four, I read in a newspaper: *Briton Caught Smuggling in Malaysia.* A few nights later, I saw Cassie, one of the girls in the camp, on the news. She'd been arrested at Kuala Lumpur airport carrying drugs. So she must have got off the island. And some of the others must have escaped too. I'm curious to know which ones. I'm sure that Bugs stayed, and Sal. I just can't stand the idea that they might turn up on my doorstep one day.

And me . . .?

I'm fine. I play video games. I smoke a little dope. I have bad dreams. I carry a lot of scars.

I like the way that sounds.

I carry a *lot* of scars.